COMES A STRANGER

He was a stranger till he came to the aid of the four Kincannons. Then Ben Lawless became their best friend. But for Mercy, Cinnamon, Caleb and Jonah it was only the beginning. When Cinnamon went missing the others had to grow up quickly if they were to find and save her. Together with Lawless and an old Lakota warrior called Shadow Wolf, they set out on an epic quest . . . and a blood-soaked showdown that none of them had foreseen.

STEVE HAYES
&
DAVID WHITEHEAD

COMES A STRANGER

Complete and Unabridged

LINFORD
Leicester

First published in Great Britain in 2011

First Linford Edition
published 2012

British Library CIP Data

Hayes, Steve.
  Comes a stranger.- -
  (Linford western library)
  1. Western stories.
  2. Large type books.
  I. Title II. Series III. Whitehead, David, *1958 –*
  813.5′4–dc23

  ISBN 978–1–4448–1345–6

Published by
F. A. Thorpe (Publishing)
Anstey, Leicestershire

Set by Words & Graphics Ltd.
Anstey, Leicestershire
Printed and bound in Great Britain by
T. J. International Ltd., Padstow, Cornwall

This book is printed on acid-free paper

For Drew and Susan

1

Mercy Kincannon stood there, shaking with fear. But she still managed to find the courage to keep the shotgun aimed at her father. 'S-Stop it, Pa,' she begged. '*Stoppit*! Please . . . don't make me shoot you!'

Elijah Kincannon was too drunk and too angry to heed his daughter's tearful warning. Without even pausing, he continued to whip his eldest son, Jonah, who lay bleeding in the mud at his feet.

Mercy started to squeeze the trigger. She had fired this Baker Model Ithaca double-barreled shotgun many times while hunting birds and small game, and seldom missed. But this wasn't a pheasant or a rabbit in front of her: it was her father; her only living parent! And much as she feared and hated him for all the drunken whippings he had given her and her siblings, she couldn't force herself to kill him . . . and her finger froze on the front trigger.

'What're you waiting for?' demanded her sister, Cinnamon. 'Do it! Pull the trigger! Shoot him . . . before he kills Jonah.'

'I'm warning you for the last time,' Mercy told her father. 'If you don't stop, I swear I'll shoot you!'

Elijah whirled around to face her, blood dripping from the buggy whip in his hand. 'You ain't gonna shoot nobody!' he raged. 'Now drop that goddamn scattergun, girl, 'fore I give you a taste of this!' He raised the whip threateningly and lurched toward Mercy.

Alarmed, she stepped back and felt her foot slip in the mud. Trying to regain her balance, she stumbled and inadvertently pulled one of the triggers.

The shotgun roared, startling everyone, and a load of 12-gauge double-ought buckshot blew a gaping hole in the side of the barn. The kick of the shotgun knocked Mercy backward and, already off-balance, she went sprawling.

For an instant no one moved.

Then Elijah, recovering first, staggered toward his daughter.

Mercy, seeing the rage in his bloodshot eyes, desperately grabbed for the dropped shotgun. But her father got to it first and kicked it out of her reach.

He stood there swaying, towering over her, pointing the buggy whip at her. 'I warned you, girl,' he said, words slurred by whiskey. 'But you wouldn't listen. You wouldn't listen an' . . . now you're gonna pay!'

As he raised the whip to strike her, a shot was fired.

The bullet cut the whip off just above Elijah's fist. Startled, he whirled around and saw a stranger peering out of the hole in the barn . . . a stranger aiming a smoking six-shooter at him.

Mercy, scrambling to her feet with the shotgun, also saw the stranger.

So did Cinnamon, Jonah and their younger brother, Caleb.

'Who the hell're you?' Elijah snarled.

'Just a stranger passin' through.'

'Then go on 'bout your goddamn business. Git!'

'Not till you quit whippin' these young folks.'

'Damn you, they're *my* children,' raged Elijah. 'I'll do what I like to 'em.'

'That's your God-given right, mister, you bein' their Pa an' all.' As he was speaking the stranger ducked his head, stepped out through the hole and stood there blinking sleepily in the bright morning sunlight. ''Course, then it'd be *my* God-given right to shoot you . . . '

He spoke softly, almost gently, but at the same time the deadly glint in his narrowed gray eyes warned that he was serious.

'You'll go straight to hell if'n do,' Elijah said.

'That'd be no surprise — for either of us.'

There was a tense silence as neither man seemed ready to back off.

'Mister,' Mercy said, her shotgun

once more aimed at her father, 'no need for you to shoot him. He's leaving — isn't that right, Pa?'

Elijah scowled at her. 'What're you sayin', girl?'

'I'm saying if you don't want buckshot for breakfast, saddle up and ride out of here. Now! And don't ever come back!'

'Damn you, girl, what right you got to tell me what to do?'

Caleb, who had been tending to his whipped brother, now glared defiantly at his father.

'She's talking for all of us, Pa. You ain't wanted!'

'He's right,' Cinnamon chimed in. 'Get on your horse and go!'

'Reckon the vote's unanimous,' the stranger said.

Elijah glowered at his four children. 'You're makin' a big mistake. You know that, don't you?'

None of them spoke.

'If'n I go, I ain't never comin' back. Y'sure that's wha' you want?'

Their angry silence assured him it was.

'Okay, suit y'selves. But don't come a-crawlin' to me when you need help, 'cause I'll spit in your miserable faces.'

'Don't worry,' Mercy said grimly. 'We'll all be six feet under 'fore that happens.'

Realizing they weren't going to change their minds, Elijah staggered on toward the barn. But a step before he got there, he stopped and looked back at them. 'Just so's you know. You think you're kickin' me out. But you ain't. You're doin' me a favor. I been wantin' to shake loose of you brats ever since your mother, God bless her, died. Now I got me a good excuse!'

He staggered into the barn. They heard him stomping around, cussing as he drunkenly tried to saddle his horse.

'I better go help him,' Mercy told her siblings, 'before he passes out and we're stuck with him again.'

'Wait,' the stranger held up his hand. 'Let me handle him. No tellin' what a man full of hate an' jug-whiskey will do next.' He walked off before they could argue, and entered the barn.

As one, the four of them watched the stranger disappear inside. Then Jonah, Cinnamon and Caleb turned questioningly to Mercy.

'Don't look at me,' she said. She brushed the bangs of her boyishly short brown hair out of her eyes, an unconscious habit she had. 'I never saw him before. And that's the truth of it.'

'What was he doing in our barn?' Cinnamon said.

'Sleeping, most likely,' Caleb said. 'Did you see all the bits of straw on his shirt and Levi's?'

'Yeah, but *why* is he sleeping there?' Jonah put in. 'That's what we got to find out.'

'Maybe he's an outlaw?' Cinnamon said, adding hopefully: 'Maybe there's a reward on his head and if we turn him in we'll be rich.'

The others looked incredulously at her.

'You'd snitch on him after the way he just helped us?' Mercy said.

Cinnamon shrugged her beautiful creamy shoulders. At almost seventeen, with long lustrous auburn hair, fine features and sultry gray-green eyes, she was much prettier than Mercy. She also spoke more precisely, as if she were more educated. But she did not have her older sister's sense of values, or determined grit and was easily the vainest and most self-centered of all the Kincannons.

'Why not,' she retorted, 'we don't know anything about him. I mean, for all we know he might have saved us so he could rape and kill us himself.'

Mercy rolled her eyes and sighed. 'You're my sister, Cinny, and I love you dearly. But sometimes, I swear I don't know who you are. Now, go heat up some water and get the salve from the cupboard.'

Angrily muttering under her breath, Cinnamon stormed into the house.

Mercy, used to her sister's tantrums,

kneeled beside Jonah. With Caleb's help, he was now sitting up in the mud, gingerly rubbing his back. His heavy twill jacket had helped to protect him against the buggy whip but he was still in pain and grimaced when he moved. 'Can you make it into the house?' she asked him.

'S-Sure, sis.'

'Help me get him up,' Mercy said to Caleb. Then, once Jonah was standing: 'Take your brother inside and make sure Cinny's put water on the stove. I'll be right along.'

Before they could question her, she hurried to the barn.

2

Mercy found the stranger leaned against the barn door, his old sweat-stained Stetson tilted slightly down over his forehead, chewing on a piece of straw as he watched Elijah tie his bed roll on behind his saddle.

'Come to gloat, have you?' Elijah growled at his daughter.

Mercy, instead of getting angry, had to fight back tears. 'Oh, Pa,' she said sadly. 'Why do you have to act so mean?'

For one infinitesimal moment her question seemed to trouble Elijah. But then he dismissed it, and her, and stepped up into the saddle.

Tears of regret now ran down Mercy's wholesome, sun-browned face. 'Pa . . . Pa, please listen to me.'

Then as he ignored her:

'Wasn't our fault Momma died, you know.'

'Never said it was.'

'Then why do you take it out on us? We loved her . . . and miss her . . . same as you.'

Her words seemed to further enrage her father. White with fury, he leaned down from his saddle until their faces were only inches apart.

'You want answers, girl, take it up with God!'

Savagely spurring his horse, he rode out of the barn.

The stranger jumped aside to avoid the charging horse, then removing his hat, scratched his shaggy light-brown hair and smiled ruefully at Mercy.

'Hope my buttin' in didn't force you to play your ace early?'

Mercy sadly shook her head and brushed the bangs out of her eyes. ''Fraid this was way overdue.'

Sensing she had more to say, he chewed silently on his straw and waited.

'It's my fault,' she said presently. 'My brothers and sister wanted to kick Pa out after the last whipping. But I talked them out of it.' She paused and gave a pained, wistful sigh. 'Being the oldest, I can remember better than they can how Pa was when Momma was alive. 'Fore she took really ill, I mean. Should have seen them together, mister, it was like in a story book.'

The stranger seemed to understand. 'Walkin' through life with the right woman is a wonderful thing,' he said. 'There was a time, way back, when I knew that feelin'.' He paused, as if savoring the memory, then: 'Sorry 'bout your Ma. What happened — fever take her?'

'Consumption.'

'Ahh,' He wrinkled his rugged, weathered face in empathy. 'Ugly way to die.'

'Very ugly. Painful, too. Near the end seemed like poor Momma never stopped coughing up blood.'

They both fell silent, each struggling with their own thoughts. Then:

'So your Pa,' the stranger said, 'he wasn't always like he is now?'

'Oh, no, just the opposite. 'Fore Momma passed, he was always laughing and teasing us . . . reading to us out of books . . . helping us with our homework.' Noticing his puzzled look, she added: 'We lived back in St. Jo' then . . . went to school just like regular children. Wasn't till after Momma died in the spring of '73 that Pa decided he could no longer live in a house where everything reminded him of her and moved us way out here . . . in an empty valley in the middle of nowhere on the wrong side of the moon, as my sister likes to say.'

The stranger smiled. Wyoming, with its vast prairie and endless horizons, reminded him of the open grasslands of Texas, where he'd grown up, and despite the presence of Cheyenne and Sioux renegades, he felt comfortable here. 'And that's when he changed — your Pa, I mean?'

'Yes. Well, not at first. I mean he was upset, like we all were. Goodness me, we all missed her terribly and felt sad and cried a lot. And that's the truth of it. But Pa, he wasn't hateful or mean. Not like now. And he *never* took a whip or a strap to us, no matter what we did — ' She broke off, shook her head and said: 'Will you listen me — carrying on like a noisy jay bird and here I don't even know your name!'

The stranger hesitated. He had ridden over a thousand miles to get away from his past and start afresh, and he wondered if it was wise to reveal who he was to a bunch of young folks that after today, he'd probably never see again. But the look of trust and honesty in girl's gentle brown eyes as she gazed up at him brushed aside his worries.

'It's Ben,' he said, offering her his hand. 'Ben Lawless.'

'Mercy Kincannon.' She shook hands, her grip firm and calloused. 'Reckon it goes without saying that I'm — we're *all* mighty grateful to meet you.'

'I'm the one who should be grateful,' Lawless said. 'My horse drowned in a flash flood just east of here an' I

14

would've spent the night splashin' around in the mud an' the rain if I hadn't spotted your barn.' He looked at the jagged, splintery hole in the wall and grinned ruefully. 'Sure don't pay to sleep late around here.'

'Oh-my-goodness,' Mercy covered her mouth in horror. 'I could have killed you!'

'Could've, would've, should've — life's too short to worry about what-ifs. I could use some coffee, though, if you happen to have a pot on the stove.'

'Follow me,' Mercy said. Turning, she led him out of the door and across the stretch of muddied dirt that separated the barn and corral from the log-walled cabin, talking as they walked. 'We were about to start breakfast when Pa rode in and got it in his mind that Jonah needed a whipping.'

'Just like that?' Lawless said, surprised. 'For no reason?'

'Oh, he had a reason. Pa *always* has a reason for no matter what he does. It's just that his reasons come out of a bottle and don't necessarily make sense to anyone but him.' She paused and shook her head at the damaged barn wall. 'Now me, I never do *anything* that doesn't make sense. You know. Like shootin' holes in a perfectly good barn that we just got through white-washing.'

Ben Lawless chuckled. It was at that moment, as he followed her into the cabin, that he first really admired her. No matter how bad life got for her, he realized, Mercy Kincannon would always find a way to laugh at it.

3

In the Kincannon family children were meant to be seen not heard. This was especially true at mealtimes and now, as head of the family, Mercy did her best to adhere to the rule.

After insisting that Lawless sit at the head of the table, she waited for her brothers and sister to take their places before somberly saying grace. She then told Cinnamon to please pass Mr. Lawless the eggs and ham, and breakfast began.

'Maybe he would prefer to have pancakes,' Cinnamon said, just to bring herself into the conversation. 'Would you, Mr. Lawless?'

'I like both,' he said, trying not to smile as Cinnamon fluttered her sultry gray-green eyes at him. She was an obvious flirt and though he guessed she was still in her teens, he had to admit

17

that he couldn't ignore how pretty she was.

'Me, too,' Caleb said. He and his brother had taken an immediate liking to Lawless; and Ben, in turn, sensing they were yearning for a father they could look up to, made an effort to be friendly to them. 'Specially buckwheats.'

'With apples and cinnamon and lots of warm maple syrup poured over 'em,' added Jonah.

Earlier Mercy had rubbed some store-bought salve over the welts on his back and now, in a clean blue shirt, except for an occasional wince as he reached for something, he did not seem to be in any pain.

'Reckon that goes without sayin',' Lawless said, winking at the boys. 'I remember once in New Mexico — the Harvey House in Deming, I think it was — hearin' a feller threaten to shoot the cook on 'count of he'd run out of maple syrup.'

Jonah and Caleb laughed, a little

raucously, causing Mercy to glare at them and loudly clear her throat. Admonished, they fell silent and went on eating.

But this was no ordinary day and Cinnamon was determined not to miss an opportunity to flirt with an attractive stranger who made her pulse quicken.

'My gracious,' she said, provocatively tossing her hair back from her face, 'I certainly envy you, Mr. Lawless. One day I too intend to get away from this hateful, uncivilized place and travel to exotic lands.'

'Deming ain't exactly what I'd call exotic,' Lawless said, again hiding a smile. 'Truth is, a few years ago, 'fore two of the big railroads linked up there, the town was mostly known for all its windmills.'

'Talkin' of windmills,' Caleb said to Mercy. 'We need to get ours fixed. Now that Pa's gone, we — '

'That's enough talk,' she interrupted. 'We don't need to bore Mr. Lawless with our daily little problems — '

'Fixin' all those missing vanes is more than a little problem,' Jonah grumbled. 'Our saw's broke and we need lumber and nails and — '

'I said, that's enough talk,' Mercy said firmly. At her stare the brothers subsided and went on eating. 'Cinny, please pour Mr. Lawless some more coffee.'

Cinnamon obeyed, trying to hide her irritation as she said sweetly, 'I do wish you wouldn't call me that. You know how I dislike it.' To Lawless, as she refilled his cup, she added: 'Don't you just hate it when people shorten your name?'

'Can't say as I've had much experience with that,' Lawless said. 'Ben is kind of short to begin with.'

'Yes, but isn't your full name Benjamin?'

'That's none of your business,' Mercy said sharply. Then to Lawless: 'You'll have to forgive us. We seldom get visitors out here, so we forget that questioning a stranger could be considered rude — even offensive.'

'No offense taken,' Lawless said affably. 'No,' he added to Cinnamon, 'it's just Ben. Always has been.'

After breakfast, while the sisters cleared the table and washed the dishes, Lawless asked Jonah and Caleb to show him their windmill. They led him to a well that was located between the corral, in which grazed four shaggy-coated horses, and a muddy pen that was home to several hogs. Towering above the well was a wooden windmill with most of its vanes missing or broken.

'Does it pump any water at all?' Lawless asked.

'Not enough to fill a thimble,' said Jonah. Though at fifteen he was a year older than his brother, he was smaller, leaner and more agile; but he had the same reddish-brown hair, merry brown eyes and engaging smile. 'Caleb an' me, we work the crank by hand.'

'If Pa hadn't broken our saw, me'n

Jonah would've fixed it ourselves — '

'There are plenty of trees in Bridger Canyon not far from here — '

'We could've cut 'em down, trimmed 'em and made new vanes — '

'But Pa, he said no every time we asked.'

'How come?' Lawless said. 'Did he want to do it himself?'

'Pa?'

'I say somethin' that tickled you,' Lawless said as the brothers laughed.

'Nah,' said Jonah. 'It's just that Pa ain't done a lick of work since we moved here.'

''Less you count bendin' his elbow at the trading post.'

'Then what was his objection to you boys fixin' the windmill?'

Jonah hesitated, as if he didn't believe it himself, then said: 'Pa had this notion that we broke the vanes off deliberately — '

''Course we didn't,' Caleb put in.

'I mean, why would we?' continued Jonah. 'Just makes more work for us.'

'But if he'd believed us then he wouldn't have had no call to whip us or make us go without supper — '

'Just like what he done with Mercy,' Jonah said. 'Pa broke some dishes one night when he come home skunk-drunk — '

' — an' he blamed her for it for months,' finished Caleb. 'Made her life miserable.'

'He is one mean ol' son-of-a-coyote,' Jonah said.

'Was,' corrected Caleb. 'Thanks to Mr. Lawless, he ain't gonna be around no more.'

'*Any* more,' Jonah corrected.

'Shut up,' Caleb said. 'I get enough of that from Mercy. She thinks it's her duty,' he added to Lawless. 'Corrects us every which way but Sunday. Makes us wash behind our ears every night, too. Has done ever since Momma passed.'

'She doesn't mean nothin' by it,' Jonah said. 'Just wants to make sure we grow up like Momma wanted.'

'Ask me,' Lawless said, 'you boys are

mighty lucky to have someone who cares that much about you.'

'Reckon we are at that,' Jonah admitted. 'Still, we're almost full-growed now an' it gets awful tiresome — ' he stopped and looked off at something.

Lawless expected Caleb to finish the sentence, a habit both boys did all the time. But Caleb was also looking off at something.

Lawless turned and looked in the same direction and saw five riders approaching out of the sun. Behind them, a distant snow-peaked mountain range made up the horizon.

'You reckon that's Pa?' Caleb asked Jonah uneasily.

'Come back to whip the skin off us? Could be.'

'If it is,' Lawless said, 'got any idea who those men are with him?'

Jonah shrugged. 'Could be anyone. Trappers, miners, gunmen — Pa knows just about everyone at the trading post.' He turned to his brother. 'Run an' tell Mercy. She'd want to know.'

'She already knows,' Caleb said, thumbing behind him.

Lawless and Jonah turned and saw Mercy, a basket of wet clothes in her hands, paused outside the door of the cabin.

Lawless, talking to the three of them, said: 'Get inside. All of you!' Not waiting to see if they obeyed, he went into the barn and reappeared shortly with a Winchester '73 and an extra gun-belt slung over his shoulder.

In his free hand he held field glasses. Raising them to his eyes he screwed the lenses around until they were clearly focused on the five riders.

'Is it him?' Mercy asked from the doorway. 'Is it Pa?'

'No.' He lowered the glasses and turned to her. 'But stay inside anyway.'

Hearing concern in his voice, she said: 'Are they Sioux?'

'Worse,' Lawless said.

'Cheyenne?'

'Scalp hunters.'

4

It took the five riders about twenty minutes to reach the Kincannon property.

By then Lawless had positioned Jonah at the cabin window with his Winchester; Mercy behind the partly open door with the shotgun; and Caleb, who was the best shot, crouched down behind a rain barrel with the family .44 caliber, brass-framed repeating Henry rifle — all with strict orders not to show themselves or start shooting until he told them to.

'What about me?' Cinnamon pouted. 'Can't I do something?'

'You got the most important job of all,' Lawless lied. 'If it gets to shootin', you're to make sure your sister and brothers don't run out of ammo.'

'Until then,' Mercy said sternly, 'keep out of sight. Last thing we need is for the likes of this trash to see someone as pretty as you. We'll never get rid of them!'

Her ego assuaged, Cinnamon sat at the table, removed the cartridges from the two extra boxes Lawless had given her and arranged them in three separates piles. She smiled as she worked, thinking that although she abhorred violence, it would be rather exciting to be the most important part of a real gun fight.

Outside, leaned against the corral fence near the water trough, Lawless made sure he had the sun behind him as he watched the riders drawing closer. While he watched, he pretended to be idly cleaning the Colt Peacemaker that belonged in the well-worn gun-belt looped over the fence.

The five riders were now less than a hundred yards away.

Lawless spat his disgust into the dirt. He knew their kind well. He had seen them all too often during the years he'd spent in the southwest and Mexico.

Border trash! Low-life men of all ages who holed up in cantinas in dirty little pueblos and towns on both sides of the U.S.-Mexican border. They were cruel, ruthless gunmen or *renegados*, as the *Rurales* called them, devoid of any decency or conscience, who robbed, raped and killed whomever and whenever they pleased.

The riders now reining up before him were no different. Big or small, they were all surly-looking, unshaven men armed with rifles, tied-down six-guns and short-barrel belly guns. This being autumn in Wyoming, they were warmly clad, with wolf-pelt vests covering their filthy red-flannel undershirts and fur caps pulled low over their ears. As Lawless had seen through his field glasses earlier, all of them had Indian scalps hanging from their saddles, like trophies, and dribbles of snuff staining their bearded lips.

The eldest was a hunched-over, white-haired patriarch of sixty-odd who had an ugly knife-scar running from his forehead to his cheek, a deformed lump of flesh that covered where his left eye used to be. He grinned at Lawless, showing broken brown teeth, and said with mock politeness:

''Hidee, mister.'

''Mornin'.'

'An' a fine mornin' it is, too.'

Lawless did not respond.

'Be 'bliged to you if'n we could water our horses.'

'Help yourselves.'

Lawless idly blew into the long barrel of the single-action Colt and then, as if satisfied it was clean, slowly began removing cartridges from the extra gun-belt and sliding them into the cylinder.

The significance of his actions didn't go unnoticed by the dismounting riders; especially the patriarch. After handing his reins to the youngest man, a tall, gaunt youth no more than twenty, he made an elaborate show of stretching and rubbing the stiffness from his back.

'Reckon I've wintered here long enough,' he grumbled. 'Time these old bones rode south to warmer climes.'

'Got a cousin feels the same way,' Lawless said. Finished loading the Colt .45 he flicked his wrist, snapping the cylinder back in place and stuck the gun into his jeans. 'Reckon that's why he stays in Texas.'

'That where you hail from, son?'

'Laredo.'

'You're a far piece from home.'

'Like my Pa used to say: 'Home is where the heart is . . . ''

'Aye,' the old man said, his little ferrety eyes taking in the surroundings.

Lawless' gaze idly wandered to the cabin, his pulse quickening as he saw Cinnamon peeking out the window. He wanted to signal to her to get back, but he knew that would only attract the scalp-hunters. So he kept still and after a few moments she disappeared. Relieved, he turned back to the patriarch, hoping that he had not caught a glimpse of the girl.

But the old man's next remark wasn't encouraging. 'Nice to have a woman to warm your feet on at night, be she white, squaw or breed.' He spat, adding to the brown dribble at the corners of his mouth. 'Can tell that boy of yourn it's all right to step out from behind the rain barrel now. As you can see, me'n my sons, we ain't meanin' you no harm.'

'Never can tell,' Lawless said, making no effort to call to Caleb.

'Wouldn't happen to have no coffee or left-over biscuits available, would you?'

'Sorry. Water's best I can do.' Lawless glanced at the four men who stood sullenly beside the horses, adding: 'Well, day's a-wastin'. So if you an' your kin are all through, I'd 'preciate it if you'd ride on so's I can finish my chores.'

The stoop-shouldered old patriarch studied him shrewdly.

'You can drop the sodbuster talk, friend. No farmer I ever knowed wore

his iron tied down way yours is. An'
that holster hangin' beside you, it didn't
get worn smooth like that from you
shootin' rabbits.'

Lawless said softly: "Least *my* 'rabbits' kept their scalps.'

'Ahh,' the patriarch said. 'So that's
what's chewin' at you?' He glanced at
the cabin. 'Got some cuddly young
breed inside, have you?'

'Like you said,' Lawless drawled,
'nice to have a woman to warm your
feet on at night, be she white, squaw or
breed.'

The old man chuckled. 'Reckon you
got me there, son.'

'Whenever you're ready, Pa,' said the
young man who'd been watering the
patriarch's grey roan. He handed the
reins to his father and climbed onto his
horse. The other men did the same.

The patriarch winked at his youngest
son, "Bliged, Joey,' then turned to
Lawless, 'Thanks for the water, mister,'
and stepped stiffly up into the saddle.
'If'n I don't head on down to your part

of the country, maybe we'll see each other again someday.'

'Never can tell,' Lawless said.

The old man grinned, sucked his teeth and spat a stream of snuff juice at a milk goat grazing nearby. It hit the goat on the ear and it jerked its head up, the bell hanging from its neck tinkling. The patriarch nodded, as if pleased with his accuracy, then spurred his horse and led his sons off across the flat, sunlit meadow beyond the cabin.

'Can come out now,' Lawless called to Caleb. 'Not you,' he added as Mercy opened the cabin door and Cinnamon appeared behind her. 'You an' your sister stay inside till I tell you.' He looked carefully around, adding: 'Could be there's a lookout glassin' us from the hills . . . or those rocks over there . . . tryin' to count exactly how many of us there are.'

''Mean they want our hair too?' Caleb said, looking after the riders.

'Silly,' Mercy said from inside.

'There's no bounty on white people's scalps.'

'No,' Lawless said, 'but there's plenty of minin' camps, saloons an' whorehouses willin' to pay top dollar for two pretty young girls, like yourselves.'

Cinnamon looked horrified. 'B-But that's slavery,' she exclaimed. She looked at Mercy and shuddered. 'I'd sooner kill myself than be fondled by a bunch of filthy old — '

Mercy cut her off. 'Hush up,' she said sternly. 'There'll be no such talk in my house!' She turned to Lawless. 'Will you be stayin' for supper or riding on?'

'Glad you brought that up,' he said. 'I need a horse. If you'll give me a price on one of those animals in the corral, I'll be happy to pay whatever you ask.'

'Those horses aren't for sale,' Jonah said, now emerging from the cabin. 'We need them to pull the wagon and for us to ride, when we go to the trading post for supplies. Right, sis?' he added to Mercy.

''Fraid so,' she agreed.

'Fair enough,' Lawless said. 'Then perhaps you'd be willin' to let me ride one of them to the post. I'm sure I can buy a horse from someone there.'

'How do we know you'll bring it back?' Caleb said.

'Mind your manners!' Mercy said sharply.

'It's a fair question,' Lawless said, adding: 'One of you can ride along with me, to make sure. How's that sound?'

'I'll go,' Cinnamon said quickly.

Mercy looked at her sister as if she were demented; while Jonah and Caleb laughed and playfully punched each other on the shoulder.

'Why shouldn't it be me?' Cinnamon said, irked by their amusement. 'I can ride just as well as any of you. And my horse is the fastest. You all said so.'

'And your brain's the smallest,' Jonah said, 'if you really can't figure out why you can't be the one to go.' Again the brothers laughed.

'Shut up!' Cinnamon told them. Then to Mercy: 'I'm sure Mr. Lawless would be happy to make sure I got back safely. Isn't that right — *Ben?*'

'*Mr. Lawless,*' Mercy said pointedly, 'isn't running this family. So quit fluttering your eyelashes at him and acting like he's your best beau.'

'Wait a minute,' Lawless said as Cinnamon started to erupt. 'May I say somethin' here?'

'Please do,' Mercy said.

'I don't need anyone to go with me. I'll pay you double for whatever you think one of your horses is worth. Then when I get back, you can return my money. An' if I don't come back, you can buy another horse and still be ahead. Does that sound fair?'

Mercy looked questioningly at her siblings, who nodded. 'Go pick out the one you want,' she told Lawless, adding: 'Do you have a saddle?'

'Nope. It was on my horse when the flood water took him.'

'Then you can borrow mine.'

''Preciate that.' Lawless opened his Levi jacket and pulled out his shirt, revealing a canvas money belt.

Counting out some bills, he handed them to Mercy. 'Three hundred sound fair?'

'More than fair.' Mercy gave the money to Cinnamon behind her. 'Put this in our money box, please. You best take some food with you,' she told Lawless. 'It's a half day's ride to the post.'

5

Lawless chose the buckskin, which belonged to Jonah, and with three of Mercy's still-warm buttermilk biscuits tucked in his saddlebag rode off toward McKenzie's Trading Post.

Though he had never been to the post, he'd gotten detailed directions from Caleb that included several easy-to-see landmarks and basically boiled down to 'keep ridin' north-west an' by mid-afternoon you'll come to it.'

'You can't get lost,' Mercy had assured him as he mounted up outside the barn. 'Not so long as you head straight for that big mountain there.' She pointed at a massive, craggy, snowy-peak that seemed to kiss the sun. 'McKenzie's is right in front of it, facing the foothills.'

Lawless, who always carried a compass, smiled his thanks. 'I'll try to make it back by tonight,' he said. 'But if I don't, it'll be early tomorrow morning.'

'Make it before breakfast,' Caleb said, 'and I'll fix you up a batch of buckwheats.'

'Ha,' Mercy scoffed. ''Mean you'll nag *me* into making them for you.'

''Mounts to the same thing,' Jonah said, winking at Lawless.

Lawless winked back, feeling great warmth for these three young people whom he barely knew, and then with a throwaway salute kicked up the buckskin and rode off.

'Sure hope he does come back,' Caleb said, looking after Lawless. 'I like him.'

'Me, too,' said his brother. 'Know what I was thinking?'

'What?'

'Wouldn't it be great if he liked us, too, an' decided he wanted to be our older brother?'

'Brother-*in-law*, don't you mean?' Caleb said with a sidelong glance at Mercy.

'Whoa, wait a minute,' she said,

catching on. 'What're you suggesting?'

'Well, you got to marry someone, sis, so why not him?'

'You like him, don't you?' Jonah said.

'Sure I like him. But liking someone doesn't mean you want to marry them.'

'No, but it's a start. I mean it's a lot better than *not* likin' them.'

''Sides,' said Caleb, 'if you don't want to marry him, I bet I know someone who does.' He grinned at his brother and they both broke into stifled laughter.

'God help me,' Mercy said, looking heavenward. 'What did I ever do to deserve you two as brothers?'

'Just lucky, I reckon,' Jonah said, and punched Caleb on the shoulder. Caleb quickly punched him back and a moment later the two of them were grappling and trying to throw the other to the ground.

'Quit fooling around,' Mercy told them. 'You've got chores to do and — ' She broke off as a thought hit her. 'Speaking of Cinny — either of you know where she is?'

The brothers stopped wrestling and looked around.

'Uh-uh,' Jonah said. 'Last time I saw her, she was over by the corral.'

'Yeah, that's where I saw her too,' Caleb said.

'Doing what?' Mercy asked.

Both brothers shrugged. 'I dunno.'

'Think! What was your sister doing?'

'Told you. I don't remember.'

'Feedin' her horse, I think,' Caleb said. 'No,' he corrected himself, 'not feedin' him. She was puttin' on his bridle.'

'What difference does it make anyways?' Jonah said. 'It ain't like you give her a lot of chores to do, like us, so — ' He stopped as his sister turned and ran into the cabin. 'What's wrong with her?' he asked Caleb.

'She's upset 'cause we asked her to marry Mr. Lawless, most likely.'

A few moments later Mercy came running out of the cabin, shouting: 'She's not in her room! Check in the barn while I see if her horse is gone!'

41

6

Bridger Canyon, named after the famous, recently-deceased mountain man and trail guide, Jim Bridger, was located a little more than halfway between the Kincannon's cabin and McKenzie's Trading Post. Two miles or so long, its sandstone walls were steep and rocky and climbed high enough to cast shadows on Lawless as he followed the stony trail that wound through it.

The buckskin he rode was a sturdy, reliable horse that lacked speed but not endurance, and Lawless kept it at a slow, steady lope that gradually ate up the miles. A chilling wind blew off the distant mountains and buffeted the white billowy clouds across the high blue sky. The autumn sun was glaringly bright but gave off little warmth, and the wind gusting through the canyon forced Lawless to keep his jacket collar pulled up around his ears.

For about an hour now he'd sensed he was being followed. But each time he looked back, he saw no one on his trail. Still, he trusted the prickling he felt on his neck whenever danger was present; and now, halfway through the canyon, he decided to make sure once and for all if he was being followed.

Ahead, the trail disappeared around a sharp bend. Once around it Lawless quickly dismounted and led his horse behind a giant boulder. There, he removed his hat, pulled his rifle from its scabbard, and peered around the edge of the boulder. Eyes fixed on the trail, he waited patiently. Several minutes passed. Still no one showed. Had he been wrong after all? Doubting it, he continued to wait and presently was rewarded by the sound of a horse approaching. He levered a round into the chamber. The noise of the horse's hoofs as they struck the stones littering the trail grew louder; closer. Lawless tensed, ready to brace his pursuer. A few more moments then a rider appeared around the bend.

Lawless stepped out into the trail, ready to shoot — then quickly removed his finger from the trigger as he recognized the rider.

'You!' he said, shocked. 'What in Sam Hill . . . ' He expelled his exasperation in an angry snort. 'Dammit, don't you realize I could've shot you?'

'Why would you do that?' Cinnamon asked. 'I'm not threatening you.'

'How am I supposed to know that? You dog a fella's trail — '

'Excuse me?'

'Follow someone — what else am I to think?'

Cinnamon arched her eyebrows and tried to look peeved. 'Do not flatter yourself, Mr. Lawless. I am not following you. I'm on my way to the trading post, same as you.'

'Like hell you are!'

'There's no need to curse.'

'No need to lie, neither.'

'I'll not dignify that with an answer,'

she said petulantly. 'Anyway, believe what you want. It makes no matter to me.'

'What I *believe*,' Lawless said, more concerned than angry, 'is that your sister would never let you ride this far by yourself. Neither would your brothers an' we both damn well know that.'

'I know nothing of the sort. Now, if you're all through shouting at me, kindly step aside so I may pass.'

'I ought to do just that,' Lawless said. 'I ought to let you ride on alone an' suffer whatever consequences are waitin' on you.'

For an instant alarm flickered in Cinnamon's sultry gray-green eyes. Then she shrugged and said indifferently: 'If you're trying to frighten me, Mr. Lawless, you're wasting your time. I'm a grown woman and I have a perfect right to go wherever I please. So, kindly get out of my way.'

Lawless obeyed. Cinnamon tapped the small, thick-coated gray horse with her heels and rode off along the trail.

Frustrated, Lawless kicked at the air and then hurried to the buckskin.

A few minutes later, when he caught up with her, she gave an annoyingly smug little smile and ignored him. Lawless wanted to put her across his knee and give her the paddling she deserved. But controlling the urge, and at the same time wondering why he cared enough about this girl — a stranger — to get angry, he rode in silence beside her.

But silence was the last thing Cinnamon wanted. And after a little she turned to him, fluttered her eyes, and said: 'I'm sorry I lost my temper back there, Mr. Lawless, but you startled me . . . gave me a scare by suddenly jumping out in front of me.'

'Forget it,' Lawless said, softening. 'I shouldn't have yelled at you. You're right: you can ride wherever you want, whenever you want. Ain't no business of mine.'

'Thank you,' she said demurely. 'I appreciate that. But I also appreciate your concern. No matter how strong or independent a woman is, she still likes it when a man shows he cares about her.'

Lawless smiled inwardly. He was in no way fooled by her glib, flirtatious advances, but nor could he deny that he found Cinnamon sexually attractive. More importantly, despite her petulance and irritating false airs, there was an alluring vulnerability about her that he found very appealing. Studying her perfect profile, he tried to decide if it was an act, something she deliberately used in an effort to make men want her or an innate emotion she had no control over. He couldn't decide. But either way, it was effective: he felt a compelling need to protect her.

'It's rude to stare, you know,' she said presently.

'Sorry.'

'Silly, I was just teasing you.'

He grunted in a way that could have meant anything.

'What were you thinking about while

you were staring?'

'Nothin'.'

'Now you sound like Caleb. It's his pet word. You could catch him with his hand in your pocket and ask him what he's doing and he'd still say: 'Uh, nothing.''

She imitated her brother's voice so perfectly that Lawless had to laugh.

'That's better,' she said, school-girlishly. 'Now we're friends again.'

They rode on. After another mile the canyon widened and its sheer rocky walls sloped down into low rolling hills that eventually opened out onto a grassy plain. Flat as a lake and bright with wildflowers, it stretched all the way to the foothills fronting the mountain range. Lawless shaded his eyes from the sun and could just make out several log buildings enclosed by a stockade.

'That the tradin' post?' he asked.

'Uh-huh.' She made a face. 'It's a revolting place. Stinks worse than a pigpen, 'specially in the winter when the snow keeps everyone inside. Then between the leaky old stove and the men smoking their pipes and cigars the air gets so smoky you can barely breathe or see across the room.'

'Is there nowhere else to buy supplies?'

'No. And according to Mr. McKenzie, who bought the place a few years ago, there never has been. Said it was originally built by French fur traders around 1840, right about the time the Oregon Trail got started. Did I say something amusing?' she asked as he chuckled.

'Uh-uh. It's just that I knew this ol' prospector once — Flapjack Thornton, his name was. Used to come down from the hills every so often and mooch drinks in this cantina in El Paso. Harmless enough, but could talk your ear off. Claimed he'd been an Indian fighter, Army scout, deputy marshal, even a mountain man. Bragged 'bout how he an' Jim Bridger used to guide wagon trains along the Oregon Trail. 'Course Bridger was dead by then so no one could call him on it.'

Cinnamon laughed and now it was her turn to stare at Lawless. 'I hate you,' she teased. 'You've led such an exciting, fascinating life and here I am stuck out in an empty valley in the middle of nowhere — '

' — on the wrong side of the moon,' he finished.

Cinnamon laughed despite herself. 'I see you've been talking to Mercy. Well, I suppose I can't blame her. I probably do say that more often than she likes.'

They rode on across the plain, following a shallow winding creek with banks purpled by clumps of lupins. The water made a happy gurgling sound as it rushed along and was so sparkling clear that trout could be seen swimming over the white pebbly bottom. Here and there stands of cottonwood gave shade to the creek, as well as to the scattered red patches of Indian Paintbrush that grew among the tall yellow-green grass.

Lawless thought he'd never seen

anything more beautiful.

'Is it like this where you come from?' Cinnamon asked.

'A few places — the high plains of Texas and New Mexico. But in the low country it's mostly dry, open scrubland. Barely enough grass to run cattle on. But in its own way just as beautiful, 'specially after a spring rain when the cactus and the desert flowers come out.'

'Now I really hate you,' she said. And this time she was half-serious.

'No need to,' Lawless replied. 'You'll find your place in the sun sooner than you think. Meantime, best thing you can do is to enjoy where you are now. Home's always borin' till you leave it. Then, oft-times you wish you'd never left.'

'Not me,' Cinnamon said bitterly. 'I'm *never* going to regret leaving here. Never ever!' They were less than a half-mile from the trading post now and she suddenly reined up and twisted in her saddle so that she faced him. 'I lied to you back there, Mr. Lawless. I *was* following you.'

'I know,' he said quietly.

'Don't hate me,' she begged. 'I hate liars. But I get so desperate and lonely at times I could kill myself. It's true,' she said, noticing his look of disbelief. 'I've really considered it.'

'Be an awful waste. 'Sides, how can you be lonely with your brothers and sister around?'

'You don't understand. *They* don't understand. They've actually grown to like it, even with Pa on their backs. But I . . . ' She paused, genuinely distraught, then said: 'Oh please, please take me with you, Ben. I must get away from here and . . . you're my only hope.'

'You don't know where I'm goin'. I ain't even sure myself.'

'Doesn't matter. I don't care. Wherever it is it can't be worse than here!'

To his surprise, Lawless realized that he was actually considering the idea.

Cinnamon, as if reading his mind,

reached out and pressed her gloved hand over his as it rested on the saddle horn. 'I know you don't love me,' she said, 'and I won't pretend that I love you. But I'm not ugly to look at and neither are you. Surely, in time, perhaps we could learn to love each other.'

It was the wrong word to use and it pushed him off the fence.

'No,' he said, gently removing her hand, 'that could never happen.'

'Why not?' she said desperately. 'Do you have a wife or a sweetheart you already love?'

'Not anymore.'

'Then what is it? Don't you find me desirable?'

He looked at her. As he did a wind moaned softly over the creek, rustling the cottonwoods and bending the wildflowers, and at the same playing with her long cinnamon-colored hair, gently blowing it around so that the loose strands shone like flames in the sunlight. He realized her skin was as white as the early snow on the mountain peaks and her eyes almost as green as the grass around their horses. She was, at that moment, the most beautiful young woman he'd ever seen.

'Well? Don't you?'

Her voice broke him out of his reverie.

'W-What? . . . Oh, sure . . . I find you very desirable.'

'Then I don't understand. Why won't you take me with you?'

'For a number of reasons.'

'Name one.'

'Well, for starters we just met. I don't know you from a plate of cold beans. On top of that, you're too young — '

'Fiddlesticks! Lots of girls get married much younger than me — '

'Not to men old enough to be their father.'

'If that doesn't bother me, it shouldn't bother you.'

'Well it does,' he lied. 'An' even if it didn't, it wouldn't matter. I don't *want* to get married — to you or any other girl. Nor do I want you taggin' along.

It's too much responsibility. An' like your sister says: That's the truth of it.'

Cinnamon didn't say anything. But the loathing in her sea-green eyes as she glared at him was almost frightening. Then, abruptly, she dug her spurs into her horse causing the startled animal to grunt and break into a gallop.

'Wait!' Lawless called after her. 'Cinnamon, hold up!' But she kept on riding and the wind blew the words back in his face.

7

By putting the spurs to the buckskin, he managed to overtake her just short of the stockade. Grabbing her reins, he pulled the laboring gray to a stop near the entrance.

The stockade gate was open and through it they could see men of all ages and descriptions milling around in front of the general store — trappers, farmers, scouts, miners, even a few Indians: once-proud warriors now sadly downtrodden and defeated.

At the rear of the compound, now that dusk was approaching, lights showed in the windows and doorways of the other buildings. Lawless heard female laughter and player-piano music coming from the last building and instantly knew why there were men eagerly lined up outside the door.

Leading Cinnamon away from the

gate, he kept close to the wall of tall, sharp-pointed timbers that had once kept the mighty Sioux and Cheyenne at bay and after a short distance reined up. 'Damn little fool,' he told her. 'What were you tryin' to prove?'

'Darn you, let go of my horse!' she demanded.

'Don't tempt me,' Lawless said, adding: 'Now you listen to me, girl — '

'No!'

'Want me to tie you up and gag you?'

'You wouldn't dare.'

'Don't bet on it.'

He sounded deadly serious and she decided not to press it.

'All right. I'm listening.'

Lawless removed his neckerchief and handed it to her. 'Tie this around your head an' make sure your hair's tucked up under it. Do it!' he said as she hesitated. Then as she reluctantly obeyed: 'Now wipe off your lip rouge.'

'Why?'

'Want me to do it for you?'

Sullenly, she took out a handkerchief

and wiped her lips clean.

Lawless leaned close, took her handkerchief and wiped the rouge from her cheeks and then buttoned up the top button of her thick woolen jacket. He then studied her and nodded. 'Better.'

'If you're trying to make me look like a boy,' she said, 'it won't work. Mr. and Mrs. McKenzie and their son Jake, they will know it's me immediately.'

'They ain't the ones I'm worried about. It's the riffraff, the drunks, drifters and scum like those scalp hunters who came by your place this mornin' — they're the ones we got to look out for.'

'Nonsense! I've been coming here with Pa and my brothers and sister for years now and nothing bad has ever happened.'

He didn't believe her. 'Exactly when's the last time you were here?'

She shrugged and avoided his gaze. 'I can't remember.'

'That's twice you've lied to me,'

Lawless said grimly. 'Do it again an' I'll feed you to the wolves!'

'M-Maybe a year ago,' she confessed.

'More likely two or three, I'll bet.' When her silence confirmed he was right, he softened his tone. 'Look, I'm not tryin' to buffalo you like your Pa. I just can't figure you out. You know you're beautiful an' you know beautiful women don't exactly grow on cactuses out here. Yet you don't seem to understand or care that by flauntin' yourself, flirtin' an' teasin' the way you do, you're invitin' all kinds of trouble.'

'All girls flirt,' Cinnamon protested. 'Where's the harm in that? Boys like it.'

Lawless thumbed at the trading post. 'You ain't dealin' with *boys* here. These are men! Not city men, not mannered men, but frontiersmen — hard, tough, whiskey-lovin' men raw and cruel as the land that everyday tries to destroy them. They got no rules, no conscience, no respect for human life — hell, they'd kill each other over a two-bit nugget or a drunken squaw.'

'So what am I supposed to do?' Cinnamon demanded. 'Stay locked up in my room for the rest of my life?'

''Course not. You got a life to enjoy, same as them. But you don't have to spit in trouble's face. God knows, it'll find you soon enough on its own.' He sighed, wondering if she had heard even one word of what he'd said. Then, 'All right now,' he said, releasing her reins, 'let's go see if I can buy me a horse.'

'Ben — '

Lawless, about to ride off, stopped and turned to her. 'Yeah?'

'Thank you.'

He studied her in the fading light. The look of sincerity in her eyes told him she meant it. He smiled, pleased as a boy out of school. It was crazy, he knew, but the need to protect her was almost overwhelming.

'Don't worry,' he heard himself say. 'Just stick close to me. You'll be fine.'

8

Except for the whore house, the general store was the most popular building at the trading post. This was not because of the large inventory of available supplies — which were so outrageously high-priced that only a needy settler or a stranded traveler could afford to purchase more than a few necessary staples. No, its popularity derived from the fact that it possessed the only entrance into the adjacent saloon.

The doorway was in the east wall of the store. Originally there had been a door. But over the years, due to the continuous stampede of thirsty patrons, all eager to swill down beer or jug-whiskey, the hinges had broken so frequently, the frustrated owner finally removed the door altogether. As a result, the loud conversations, drunken arguments and raucous laughter often drowned out the quieter voices of the customers in the store.

It was no different now as Lawless and Cinnamon entered from outside. A ruckus in the saloon hid the tinkling of the bell over the door, enabling them to approach the display counter without the clerk hearing them.

'Well,' Cinnamon said impatiently as the young man continued tallying a stack of invoices. 'Are you going to serve us or not, Jake McKenzie?'

Startled, the clerk jumped and knocked over the ink well with his elbow. 'Aww, hell!' he exclaimed. Grabbing a cloth he frantically began mopping up the spilled ink. 'F-Forgive me, Miss Kincannon. Reckon I didn't hear you come in.'

Cinnamon laughed. 'I gathered that,' she said, enjoying his panic. 'Good thing for you your father's not here. He'd deduct that ink from your wages.'

Immediately the clerk looked uneasy. 'You won't tell him, will you, Cinny? Pa already charged me a nickel this week for breakin' one of the liquorice jars.'

'You call me Cinny again,' she threatened, 'I'll not only tell him about the ink but I'll say I saw you stealing money from the cash drawer.'

'Y-You wouldn't — ' Jake McKenzie paled at the thought. He was a tall, angular young man with dark curly hair, dark bearcub eyes and a likable smile. He wasn't smiling now though; in fact he looked so worried that Lawless felt sorry for him.

'Don't worry, young fella. This won't go no further. Got my word on it.'

'Thanks, mister.' Jake frowned at Cinnamon. 'How come you got your hair all covered up an' your lips are so pale? I almost didn't recognize you.'

Cinnamon blushed. 'I must look simply awful,' she began.

'Oh no, Miss Kincannon, you could never look awful. Not to me — '

'All right, all right,' Lawless cut in. 'Let's get down to business. I want to talk to your father, son — '

'Oh, goodness me,' Cinnamon interrupted, 'where are my manners. Jake, this is my friend, Mr. Lawless. He's here to buy a horse.'

Jake beamed. 'Mister, you've come to the right place. Just a while back Pa was talking to these men who had some horses for sale.'

'Where are they now?' Lawless asked.

'Horses are in the corral out back — the men,' Jake pointed through the doorway at three ill-clad, stubble-faced misfits who sat at a plank table passing a jug around. 'That's them there.'

'An' your Pa, where's he?'

'Home, eatin' supper. But I can fetch him if you like.'

'I'll see the horses first,' Lawless said.

'Sure,' Jake said. 'Can go out the back door, if you want,' he pointed at a door at the rear of the large, warm, wood-smelling room. 'Saves goin' all the way 'round the store.'

''Bliged,' Lawless said. Then to Cinnamon: 'C'mon.'

'Would it be all right if I stayed here?'

64

she asked. 'I hate horses.'

Lawless hesitated. Instinct told him to say no. But the ruckus in the saloon had quieted and the only folks in the store were two women in bonnets who were examining a bolt of cloth in the corner.

'I promise I won't go anywhere,' Cinnamon said. 'I'll stand right here in this spot with Jake till you come back.'

'I'll see nothin' happens to her, Mr. Lawless,' Jake said. 'Honest.'

Lawless hesitated another moment then reluctantly nodded. 'I'll hold you to that, son.' Giving Cinnamon a final warning look not to move, he opened the door and stepped outside.

Jake grinned. 'Sure glad he let you stay, Cinny. Yesterday, Pa got in a shipment of candy. Guess what was in it — milk chocolate, come all the way from St. Louis. I hid one of the bars in the storeroom, 'specially for you.'

'I can't go into the storeroom,' Cinnamon said. 'Didn't you hear me just now? I promised Ben I wouldn't move from this spot.'

'I heard,' Jake said. 'But, well, I figured since the storeroom's so close'n all . . . ' He paused and glanced at a door behind the counter that was a few steps away before adding: 'I mean, we'd only be gone a second or two.'

'Last time you kissed me,' Cinnamon reminded, 'it lasted a lot longer than a second or two. More like a whole minute.'

'You didn't seem to mind.'

'Didn't say I minded. Just said . . . Did you *really* save me a chocolate bar, Jake McKenzie, or are you just fibbing so's you can kiss me?'

'What do you think?' he said indignantly. Then as she looked uncertain: 'Pa says it's the best chocolate in the whole the world. Says it comes from some foreign place called Bel . . . uh . . . gum.'

'Bel-gum?' She frowned disparagingly. 'Do you mean *Belgium?*'

'Maybe. It's 'cross the ocean somewheres.'

Cinnamon chewed her lip, tempted. 'I *do* love chocolate,' she admitted.

★ ★ ★

Outside, in the near-dark behind the store, Lawless stood with his elbows leaned on the fence, studying the six horses corralled in front of him. All were bays. All were rawboned and sturdy. All had recently been branded.

No, he thought as he moved along the fence and got a closer look at one of the horses, not branded — *rebranded*! Bending down, he peered between the bars at the brand burned on the bay's rump: D.B. He thought a moment, peered even closer and tried to make out the faint markings under both letters.

'U.S.' he said suddenly. 'Dammit, they're army horses!'

Hearing footsteps behind him, he whirled, hand dropping to his holstered six-gun.

'Easy, mister, easy.' The man talking

stopped and raised his hands. 'No call for gunplay.' He was a big hulking man in a long wolf-pelt coat, with a ratty beard and long matted hair poking out from under his fur cap. Keeping his hands up, he grinned at Lawless. 'Just come out to check on the horses.'

Lawless tucked the thumb of his right hand into his gun-belt, and remained ready to draw at the slightest provocation. 'Next time,' he drawled, 'might be wise to make some noise 'fore you come up behind a feller in the dark.'

'Maybe if'n I'd seen you there, mister, I would've. But you bein' hunkered down an' all . . . ' He shrugged his massive shoulders and grinned again. 'You'n me, we on church-meetin' terms now?'

Lawless said: 'These your horses?'

'Me'n my partners, yeah. You interested in buyin' one?'

'Maybe — *if* you got a bill of sale on him.'

'Ain't our word good enough?'

'For me, sure. But maybe not for a

patrol of nosy blue bellies.'

'These ain't army horses, if that's what you're gettin' at.'

'I'm glad to hear that,' Lawless said. ''Cause I was noticin', all of them have got calluses right 'bout where those little bitty cavalry saddles rub against their withers.'

'You got sharp eyes, mister.'

'They come in useful,' Lawless said, 'when you're a stranger ridin' through soldier-boy territory.'

The big man didn't say anything. Nor did he move. Yet Lawless sensed the tension building between them and got ready to jerk his iron.

'Well, can't blame a fella for not wantin' to get his neck stretched,' the big man said. He grinned, revealing bad teeth. 'Tell you what, friend. You decide you wanna buy one of them horses, come'n find me. I'll be inside liftin' a jug with my partners.'

He walked past Lawless, close enough for Ben to smell the sweat and stench of his body reeking through his

69

fur coat, and disappeared into the dark walkway separating the store from the whore house.

Lawless waited, ready to draw if the man suddenly reappeared. But he didn't and Lawless turned back to the horses, wondering as he looked them over if it was worth the risk of being hung in order to have the freedom of a horse under him. Deciding it wasn't, he turned from the corral, hearing as he did a single, frightened scream inside the store.

Running to the back door he jerked it open, not knowing what he might see but expecting the worst.

What he wasn't expecting was for Cinnamon to stumble backward into his arms. He caught her, managed to keep his balance, and saw the three horse-traders leering at him from the crowded doorway. Behind them stood their partner, the big man he'd just been talking to, a jug of whiskey now tilted on his shoulder.

Rage boiled through Lawless. He had

to fight not to gun down all of them. 'You all right?' he grimly asked Cinnamon.

She nodded, pale and trembling, holding the front of her coat together.

Lawless gently set her down. His kerchief was gone and her auburn hair now hung raggedly about her shoulders. She was breathing heavily as if she'd just fought someone off.

'What happened?' he asked, through gritted teeth.

'They were t-trying to force me to kiss them . . . ' She wiped the back of her hand across her lips and grimaced. 'Jake tried to stop them, but they — '

'Girl's got it all wrong, Reb,' the smallest man said. The leader of the group, he wore a greasy buckskin shirt, leggings tucked into his boots, and an old blue Union Officer's cap pulled low over his eyes. 'We didn't mean her or the boy no harm. We was just funnin' with 'em — '

'He's lying,' Cinnamon said. 'He ripped open my coat and when I begged him to stop, he laughed and grabbed my wrists, said he was going to make me feel like a real woman. That's when Jake tried to stop him. But he only laughed again and knocked Jake down. Then those two' — she indicated the two men flanking the big man — 'started kicking him.'

'Ain't how it happened at all,' the leader said. 'Her coat was already tore open when she an' the boy come bustin' out of the storeroom. All we done is try to pleasure her — you know, finish off what the boy started — '

He stopped as a groan came from the floor.

'Help him up,' Lawless said, hand on his gun.

The three men looked at the leader. He saw murder in Lawless' flinty eyes and quickly nodded. Together, they dragged Jake to his feet and mockingly brushed him off. His lips were bruised and blood trickled from his nose.

'You okay, son?'

Jake nodded and gingerly felt his nose.

'Is it broke?' Lawless asked.

'Reckon not.'

'See,' the leader said, smiling. 'Like I tol' you, no harm done, Reb.'

'Don't call me that,' Lawless said grimly. 'I never wore the gray.'

'But your sympathies rode with the South, right? Else you wouldn't be callin' the army blue bellies.'

Lawless silently cursed himself for the slip.

'What about the horses?' the leader persisted. 'My partner, here, says you're interested in one.'

'Not anymore,' Lawless said.

'He thinks we stole 'em from the army,' the big man said.

The leader lost his smile. 'Now where'd you get a fool notion like that from?'

'Reckon I know a runnin' iron when I see it.'

'So do I, Reb. But this brandin' was done legal. We *bought* them horses from the army. Hell, I still got me the bill of sale signed by the agent at Fort Russell. It's in my saddle bags. Be happy to show it you anytime.'

'No need,' Lawless said. 'I've decided to keep the horse I got. C'mon,' he said to Cinnamon, 'time we started back.'

'Do we have to?' she protested. 'Couldn't we stay here tonight and then go home in the morning. I'm awfully tired.'

'There's a loft over the livery stable,' Jake said. 'Pa uses it to store hay sometimes. I bet he'd let you sleep there if you asked him.'

'Please, Ben,' Cinnamon pleaded. 'It'd be better for the horses, too.'

Lawless looked at the four men, who had stepped back but were still listening to the conversation. Realizing he and Cinnamon would be easy targets in the dark, he nodded to Jake. 'Reckon it'd be okay — long as your father agrees.'

'I'll go get him,' Jake said. 'Have him meet you at the stable.' He hurried off.

'No hard feelin's, I hope?' the leader

said, extending his hand to Lawless. 'I mean maybe we treated the girl a mite rougher than we should've, but, hell's fire, liquor sometimes does that to a man.'

Lawless ignored his hand. 'Any of you get within breathin' distance of her again,' he warned all of them, 'I promise you it won't end in words.'

He guided Cinnamon past the four men and out the front door.

9

A few minutes later, outside the livery stable, the owner of the trading post introduced himself to Lawless and apologized to Cinnamon for the 'boorish behavior of a few drunken ruffians!'

A small, balding man of sixty Andrew McKenzie spoke with a noticeable Canadian-Scottish burr, strutted like a rooster, and had a reputation for never backing down from anyone. 'But I swear by The Bruce, Miss Cinnamon, ye'll nae have to worry about their likes anymore. I kicked the bullies out — them and their infernal horses.'

'Thank you, Mr. McKenzie. That was most kind of you.'

'Think nothing of it, lass. In bygone years this trading post earned a bad reputation — perhaps deservedly so — but I can assure ye, Mrs. McKenzie and I are doing our best to change all that. Respectability is our goal, and by all that's holy, Agnes and I aim to achieve that goal. As for the use of my loft tonight,' he said to Lawless, 'you and Miss Cinnamon are most welcome to it.'

''Preciate that, Mr. McKenzie,' Lawless said, reaching into his pocket. 'If you'll just tell me how much — '

'No, no, no, there'll be no talk of money 'tween us, sir. After the distasteful experience the poor lassie had to endure, why even a canny businessman like m'self would be hard-pressed to justify any payment. What's more, if ye need anything, like extra blankets or a wee nip of the heather to keep ye warm, just say the word and I'll have young Jake take care it.'

'Thanks,' Lawless said. 'But we'll be fine.'

'I wish ye both goodnight then,' McKenzie said. He started to walk away then stopped and, concerned, looked back at Cinnamon. 'Aye, I almost forgot. Your daddy, has he come upon ill health?'

'Father? I, uh . . . He . . . '

Cinnamon hesitated, uncertain how to answer.

'Elijah's fine,' Lawless said. 'Why do you ask?'

'Well, now, I couldnae help noticing his absence today. This is the first time in many a month that he has not propped up the bar, so to speak.'

'Ahh,' Lawless said. 'Makes sense.'

'F-Father's with his grandmother back in St. Jo',' Cinnamon blurted. 'I mean his mother . . . *my* grandmother. She's old and feeling right poorly.'

'So he went to look after her? Well, bless his bonnie heart for that,' McKenzie said. 'As ye well know, Elijah has a dark side to him, and can be difficult to deal with at times. But I've always suspected that beneath his harsh ways and thirst for spirits there lived a kindly, gentle man.'

Not trusting himself to answer, Lawless smiled, nodded goodnight and led Cinnamon into the barn.

That night they spread their bedrolls atop the scattering of hay that covered the loft floor and tried to fall asleep.

It wasn't easy. The loft had no windows, but it did have a floor-to-ceiling opening through which bales of hay could be delivered or tossed out. There was no door to shelter them from the cold or the wind, or the bright moonlight that seemed to shine in Cinnamon's her eyes no matter where she moved her bedroll. Neither could it keep out the sound of the player-piano in the vestibule of the whore house which played the same three songs non-stop; nor the raucous laughter of the men drinking in the saloon, who got drunker and rowdier as the night wore on.

And in the rare moments of silence, Cinnamon's stomach never stopped growling. Embarrassed by its unladylike rumbling, she finally sat up, glared across at Lawless and grumbled: 'I *told* you we should've had supper. I'm starving.'

About to tell her to stop complaining, Lawless remembered the buttermilk biscuits Mercy had insisted on giving him. Rising, he dug them out of his saddlebag and keeping one biscuit for himself, gave the other two to Cinnamon.

'Eat,' he told her. 'Then shut up and go to sleep.'

'You don't have to be rude, Mr. Lawless.' She petulantly turned her back to him so he wouldn't see her wolfing the biscuits down. 'May I have some water,' she said when she was finished.

'Sure. Here,' he tossed her his canteen.

Disappointed that he hadn't brought it to her, she drank greedily from it. 'Why are you being so hateful?' she said as she replaced the cap. 'It wasn't my fault those horrible beasts attacked me.'

'Maybe not. But like I warned you earlier — give this kind of trash the wrong impression an' they'll make you pay for it every time.'

He expected her to protest, or deny that she had been in the storeroom with Jake, but she didn't. She sat there, back against the wall, in thoughtful silence. Hoping that she might actually be learning, he rolled a smoke, flared a match to it and leaned against his saddle.

'Know what Caleb did once?' she said, trying to keep the conversation going. 'He stole Father's pipe and tried to smoke it in the barn.' When Lawless didn't respond, she added: 'Used up almost a whole box of matches, and then, when it kept going out on him, he got so mad he kicked the lamp over. It broke and oil spilled on the hay and, next thing he knew, the barn was on fire.'

'That must've pleased your Pa.'

Cinnamon frowned, troubled by the memory. 'He whipped Caleb till he couldn't stand and finally passed out. My brother was only ten then, and if it hadn't been for Mercy, who drove Father away with the pitch fork, I think he would have gone on whipping Caleb till he was dead.'

Lawless sighed, disturbed by the incident. As a boy his old man had taken a belt to him on numerous occasions. But never to inflict more than justified punishment for whatever act of mischief his son had done. For a father to whip his boy senseless, for any reason, even the tragic death of a beloved wife, was unfathomable to Lawless; especially a father who apparently was religious enough to give all his children Biblical names!

'When your mother passed,' Lawless said as a thought hit him, 'did your Pa keep on readin' the Bible?'

'No,' Cinnamon said. 'He hated God after Momma died. He stopped saying his prayers too. Insisted we do the same. We didn't of course — we just said them when he wasn't around. Why?'

'Just wonderin'.' Then as another thought came to him: 'Ain't none of my business, mind, but how come you don't have one — a religious name, I mean?'

'I did. According to Mercy, before I was born my folks planned on calling me Ruth — if I was a girl, that is.'

'What changed their mind?'

'This,' she said, indicating her silvery-tinted auburn hair. 'Soon as Father saw me in Momma's arms, and noticed all my red hair, he clapped his hands and said, 'Cinnamon! It looks just like cinnamon!' and that's what they ended up calling me.'

'Fits,' Lawless said. 'Ruth ain't a name that would've suited you.'

Cinnamon didn't seem to hear him. 'Wish I'd brought my brush,' she murmured. 'I hate it when my hair gets all messy and tangled like this.'

'One night won't kill you,' Lawless said. 'Come mornin', when you get back home, you can brush it all you like.'

She looked at him, face pale and lovely in the moonlight. 'I meant,' she said quietly, 'I wanted it to look nice for you.'

Lawless felt his mouth go dry. He swallowed, but it didn't help.

'It's going to be cold tonight. Want me to come and cuddle up to you, Ben?' She was already on her knees, ready to crawl across the hay to him when he quickly held up his hand.

'I don't think that's a good idea,' he managed to say.

Cinnamon laughed softly. 'Poor Ben,' she mocked. 'Why won't you admit how much you want me? You do, don't you?' she added. 'I can tell by the way you look at me.'

'Dammit, girl, go to sleep!'

'No,' she said, still amused. 'I don't want to. I'm going to lay here all night, wide awake, thinking about how much you want to hold me . . . and kiss me.'

Lawless didn't answer. But it was a long, hard night for him.

10

A rooster crowing awakened Lawless shortly before dawn. At once, challenging cries came from other roosters scattered about the trading post.

Lawless removed his hat from over his face, peered at the lavender-gray sky outside the doorway and shivered. It had gotten bitterly cold during the night, making him glad that he'd left his undershirt on, and now off in the distance he could hear thunder rumbling, A storm was approaching. That meant it could rain during their ride back to the cabin and remembering how yesterday he'd lost his horse in the flash flood, he wondered how dangerous it would be riding through Bridger Canyon. Damn, he thought. Why had he let the girl dissuade him from leaving last night?

Mind on Cinnamon, he rose up on

his elbows, yawned, rubbed the sleep from his eyes and looked across the loft at her — or where he expected to see her sleeping.

Only she was not there. Her canvas bedroll and crumpled woolen blanket lay atop the hay; so did her well-worn saddle with her initials burned into the cantle. But no Cinnamon!

Guessing she had gone to use the toilet behind the stable, Lawless yawned again, stretched lazily and then tugged on his jeans. Realizing he also needed to relieve himself, he finished dressing, pulled on his boots and jacket, buckled on his gun-belt and went to the wooden ladder that descended to the barn.

Only, like Cinnamon, it was not there.

'Sonofabitch!' Hunkering down, he peered into the gloom below and saw the ladder lying on the straw-covered floor. Blaming Cinnamon for somehow knocking it down and not bothering to stand it up again, he turned his back to the doorway and lowered himself to his full length, hung there briefly, then released his grip and dropped to the floor. It was only a few feet and he landed upright.

Taking a moment to lean the ladder against the edge of the loft, he went outside.

It was still dark. Thunderheads now dominated the lavender-gray sky. The distant thunder continued to rumble but the roosters had stopped crowing, and the compound was strangely quiet. Lawless started toward the old wooden outhouse — then abruptly stopped as he noticed the door was open. It swung slowly back and forth in the cold, stiffening breeze, creaking ominously, banging against the frame each time it closed.

Something cold and greasy turned over in the pit of Lawless' stomach. Where the hell was Cinnamon if she wasn't in the outhouse? Was the ladder laying on the floor no accident? And if so, who was responsible for it — those four horse thieves who had cornered her in the store?

Questions raced through his mind. He glanced about him. Nothing stirred in the fading darkness. But a light showed in the window of the general store suggesting someone was up. He hurried to the front door. It was locked. He pounded on it and heard footsteps approaching. A lock slid aside and the door opened to reveal Andrew McKenzie — a very *angry* Andrew McKenzie, who had hurriedly dressed in the dark, and now glared at the shadowy figure silhouetted against the gray dawn light.

'So!' he said. 'Got cold feet, did ye? Well, don't expect that to win ye any forgiveness from me, lad — '

'Mr. McKenzie,' Lawless stepped into the light, 'it's me — Ben Lawless.'

The little Scotsman stared at him disbelievingly, mouth agape.

'Who did you expect — your son?'

McKenzie closed his mouth and sagged as if defeated. Then, tight-lipped, he turned and went to the counter, picked up a note and handed it to Lawless.

Lawless walked to the hurricane lamp flickering beside the open, empty cash-drawer and read what was written on the back of an invoice. Hastily scribbled by McKenzie's son, Jake, it briefly explained that he and 'Cinny' had gone to Cheyenne and would not be back. They were in love and wanted to spend their lives together. He hoped his father and mother would forgive him, as he loved them very much, and added that Cinny would write to her brothers and sisters as soon as they were settled in Cheyenne.

The note ended with an apology from both of them for leaving without telling anyone — 'but we knew if we told you, Pa, you and Mr. Lawless would only stop us.' It was signed by Cinnamon and Jake, followed by a row of x's for kisses. At the bottom was a postscript saying that they would leave the wagon beside the tracks where the train picked them up.

Lawless felt as if he'd been punched in the gut. 'Any idea how long ago they left?' he asked McKenzie.

'I cannae say for certain, Ben, but it can't be more than ten minutes ago.' He thumbed at the flickering lamp, adding: ''Twas almost out of oil when I went to bed last night, so — ' As if on cue, the wick fluttered weakly and started to dim.

Lawless was already striding to the door. 'I'm goin' after them!'

'I'll come with ye,' McKenzie said. 'Be faster than me trying to describe how to get to the railway tracks.'

★ ★ ★

The recently-installed spur that connected to the main Union Pacific line that led to Cheyenne was a little more than two miles from the trading post. The trail was well-marked, mostly flat, and under normal conditions could be reached by horse or wagon in about fifteen minutes. But on this particular morning as Lawless and McKenzie spurred their mounts in the direction of

90

the tracks, conditions were far from normal.

Storm clouds blackened the sky. Loudening thunder cracked overhead and forked lightning zigzagged down from the heavens, each time briefly turning the prairie bright as day.

Then there was the rain. Gusts of wind lashed the downpour against their faces, forcing them to squint, and turned the trail into a quagmire. Swift-moving waves of muddy water swept across in front of them, carrying uprooted trees and bushes and rocks as it threatened to wash everything away.

Still they spurred their struggling horses on, whipping them with the reins when they started to lag, and eventually reached the railroad tracks. Overhead the windblown storm clouds hid the approaching dawn, keeping everything dark and preventing the two men from knowing how long the ride had taken them or if the train had already come and gone.

'Where's the pick-up point?' Lawless

shouted, trying to be heard above the storm.

McKenzie didn't try to answer. He signaled for Lawless to follow him and rode east alongside the tracks. The sheeting rain made it impossible to see more than a short distance ahead; but after a quarter mile or so, Lawless managed to make out an overturned wagon in a small clearing in front of them. The team had bolted, breaking off the yoke, and all four wheels were half-buried in the mud.

Lawless wiped his eyes with his hand, desperately trying to see if Cinnamon or Jake had been thrown clear or were trapped under it. But he could see no sign of them and his hopes died. Their only chance of survival, he realized, was if they had gotten off the wagon before it flipped over then boarded the train and were now on their way to Cheyenne —

'There they are!' McKenzie yelled, pointing, and spurred his horse forward.

Lawless followed, his horse slipping and sliding as it tried to keep its footing in the mud. As he got closer he saw two sodden, hunched-over figures huddled under the back of the wagon. The drop-down gate was smashed but both sides were still intact, saving them from being crushed.

Relieved and at the same time furious at them, he quickly dismounted. The rain hammered against his drenched slicker. Keeping his head turned away from the slashing rain, he tied the reins to one of the wagon wheels. Then, hunkering down beside McKenzie, who was already kneeled in a deepening river of mud beside his son, Lawless leaned forward and ducked his head under the wagon. His face was now only inches from Cinnamon.

About to admonish her for running away and risking her life, he stopped as he saw how panicked she was.

Melting, he instead reached out both arms, and with a frightened sob she flung herself into them. 'It's okay,' he soothed, his words lost in the storm. 'I've got you. You're safe now.' Keeping his arms around her, he moved back, got his feet under him and picked her up.

Nearby, McKenzie was helping his son to his feet. He gestured for Lawless to go ahead.

Lashed by wind and rain, Lawless carried Cinnamon to his horse. She clung desperately to him, sobbing hysterically. Alarmed, he stopped and looked down at her wet, upturned face. Her sea-green eyes gazed up at him through her matted, bedraggled hair. There was nothing sultry about them now — just fear and shock. Then, as if suddenly recognizing him, she stopped sobbing. But her lips kept moving and he realized she was repeating something over and over. He couldn't hear what she was saying above the noise of the storm, but it didn't matter. The fact that she was alive and unharmed made everything else seem insignificant.

11

By the time the four of them arrived back at the trading post, the worst part of the storm had moved on. The thunder had long since faded into the distance, taking most of the wind and rain with it.

Lawless, anxious to give his weary horse a rest, accepted Mrs. McKenzie's offer to cook breakfast for him and Cinnamon. Before they ate, though, Agnes insisted on boiling enough water for them to wash the mud from themselves. 'You can use our tub,' she told them. 'I wouldn't trust what you might find crawling in the communal bathhouse.'

Lawless let Cinnamon bathe first and while he was awaiting his turn he gave Agnes money and asked her to pick out a dress for 'Cinny.' She happily obliged, her choice of a yellow gingham print with white cuffs and collar bringing a gasp of delight from Cinnamon. Up until then she had been very subdued and seemingly ashamed of herself. She had not spoken to Lawless during the ride to the trading post, and once there had done her best to avoid meeting his gaze. He did not press her to speak, since there was very little he could tell her that she hadn't already found out for herself; but later, when they were eating breakfast in the McKenzie kitchen, he sensed there was something important that she needed to get off her chest.

'If you got somethin' to tell me,' he said quietly, 'now'd be a good time to spit it out.'

Cinnamon blushed, and keeping her eyes lowered said: 'I was wondering . . .'

'If I'm gonna tell Mercy and your brothers what happened?'

She nodded.

'Would you . . . if you were me?'

She struggled to find an answer. 'I

96

don't know,' she said at last. 'Maybe.'

'If I don't, somebody else sure as hell will. 'Less it's different in Wyoming, a tale like this would be on everybody's lips in most towns in Texas or New Mexico.'

'It's no different here,' she admitted. 'Or back in St. Jo'. Gossip spreads faster than a fever . . . always has.'

Lawless thought a moment. Then as he wiped up the last of the egg yolk on his plate with a biscuit, he said: 'How 'bout I let you tell them?'

Cinnamon's eyebrows arched with surprise. 'You'd trust me to do that?'

'Why not? Way I look at life, all of us take a wrong step now an' then. 'Long as we learn from it, I figure we deserve a second chance.'

Beaming, Cinnamon jumped up, came around the table and hugged him. 'Oh, thank you, thank you, Ben.'

'You're right welcome,' he said. Her exuberant display of affection slightly embarrassed him. But at the same time he enjoyed her arms about him, as well as the fragrance of the bath salts Agnes McKenzie had sprinkled in the tub water. 'But do me a favor — wait till after I've gone. Okay?'

'If that's what you want, yes.' She kissed him on the cheek, adding: 'You're the sweetest man I ever knew.'

Lawless grinned despite himself. 'There's some I've known who might take exception to that.'

★　★　★

The sun peered out from behind the clouds as the two of them rode into Bridger Canyon. Lawless reined up and looked at the steep cliffs towering above them.

'From here on in,' he warned Cinnamon, 'keep a sharp lookout for fallin' rocks. A rain like we had can wash away most of the dirt holdin' them in place . . . then sometimes the slightest sound or even a bird settlin' on 'em can break them loose an' bring them rollin' down on top of you.'

She nodded. 'I'll watch out,' she

promised. 'And you do the same thing. Otherwise, I might end up having to save *your* life.'

They rode on, letting their horses carefully pick their way over the stones and rocks and other debris that now covered the muddy trail.

An hour passed. The clouds had thinned out and the sun felt warm on their shoulders. Ahead, in the near-distance, they could see the end of the canyon and beyond the V-shaped cliffs, the broad grassy plain separating them from their destination.

'Ben . . . ?'

'Uh-huh?'

'Will I ever see you again?'

'I wouldn't doubt it,' Lawless said. 'I ain't exactly sure where I'm headed, or how far I'll have to ride 'fore I find what I'm lookin' for bu — '

'What *are* you looking for, if you don't mind my asking?'

'Wish I knew,' he said wistfully. 'I do know this, though: I'll know it when I see it — '

He broke off abruptly as he saw sunlight glinting on a rifle high among the rocks to their right — but before he could warn Cinnamon, a shot rang out.

Lawless felt the bite of the bullet.

It was the last thing he remembered as he pitched from the saddle.

12

When Lawless next opened his eyes everything was a blur. He felt numb all over and could hear voices that seemed to be a long way off. He blinked, trying to clear away the haze; then when he still couldn't see, he tried to rub his eyes. But he hadn't the strength to lift his arms. He could move his legs a little under what felt like a blanket, but when he went to sit up he felt so nauseous he had to lie back down. Calmly, he blinked a few more times. Gradually the blur faded, everything became clear and he could see the world around him.

He lay on a cot, covered by a gray wool blanket, in a small log-walled bedroom. The ceiling was made of logs too, suggesting he was in some kind of cabin. He went somewhere briefly, where everything was silent and dark, and when he returned the pain had lessened to a dull, throbbing ache. He tried to twitch his ears but they were bound tightly to his head by some kind of cloth or bandage.

Guessing that he had injured his head in some way, he closed his eyes and tried to recall what had happened prior to all this. Blurred images came and went, and he vaguely remembered hearing a shot. But before he could be sure, or bring the images into focus . . . someone entered the room.

Hearing footsteps approach alongside the cot, he opened his eyes and gingerly turned to look at the person, his heart jumping as he recognized . . . Mercy!

At the same instant she saw that he was awake and gave a gasp of joy, followed by an excited scream. 'Jonah! Get in here! Quick! H-He's awake!'

★ ★ ★

Later, as he sat propped up by pillows, sipping spoonfuls of hot soup that Mercy fed him, Lawless listened as she

102

and Jonah told him what happened four days ago.

'*Four days?*' Lawless exclaimed.

'Uh-huh. You've been asleep till just a little while back.'

Shocked, he gazed about him. 'Where am I?'

'The trading post. This is Jake's — Mr. McKenzie's son's — bedroom.' Mercy went on to explain that when he and Cinnamon didn't show up at the cabin that night or all of the following day, as expected, she and her brothers got worried. Leaving Caleb behind to take care of things, she and Jonah went looking for them. They had hoped to meet Lawless and Cinnamon on the trail. But when with each mile that didn't happen, the two of them glumly pressed on until they reached Bridger Canyon.

The storm had long departed, but the trail was still muddy and covered with fallen debris. A normally dry riverbed that ran parallel to the trail was still flooded so that it spilled over its banks in places. And every now and then parts of the rain-sodden cliffs suddenly gave way, and shale and rocks came slithering down to imperil the lives of any living creature below.

After a particularly large boulder bounced its way to the bottom, smashing the rocks it landed on, Jonah reined up and told his sister that they had to turn back. It was too dangerous to go on. Mercy didn't argue. Instead she told him to stay put while she looked around to make sure Cinnamon and Lawless were not somehow trapped in the canyon, and rode off.

Angry with her, and himself for lacking her courage, Jonah spurred his horse after her. He soon caught up with her. But instead of scolding him for not obeying her, as he expected, she smiled as if she had known all along how he'd react.

They rode for about fifty yards and then found their way blocked by a rockslide. Twenty feet high in some places, much less in others, the barricade stretched from one side of the canyon to the other.

'Maybe they got this far an' then turned back?' Jonah said.

If Mercy heard him, she showed no sign of it. Dismounting, she handed her reins to her brother and carefully picked her way over the debris to a low spot in the barricade.

Jonah watched as she climbed up the rocks; then, seeing what was on the other side, gave a startled gasp and cried: 'J-Jonah! Jonah, c'mere. Quick!'

Dismounting, he ran to the barricade, asking, 'What is it?' several times. His sister didn't answer. He scrambled up and over the rocks and looked down. Mercy was kneeled on the ground beside a body. He panicked. 'Is it — Cinny?'

'No — Mr. Lawless!'

Jonah scrambled down the rocks and joined his sister. Lawless lay on his side, motionless, eyes closed, the whole left side of his face caked with dried blood that had flowed from a deep gash along his temple. 'Is he dead?'

'I don't know. I th-think so . . . ' She grasped Lawless' wrist and felt for a pulse. 'I can't feel anything.'

''Cording to Pa, you can always tell if a person's dead by their eyes.'

'How?'

'They creep open — '

'They do?' Mercy looked doubtful. 'You sure?'

Jonah shrugged. 'That's what Pa said.'

They rolled Lawless onto his back and peered at his eyes. Both lids were shut and caked with dried blood. 'If Pa's right,' Mercy said, 'he's got to be alive.'

'He is! He is!' Jonah exclaimed as Lawless' eyelids twitched for an instant then grew still. 'I just saw 'em move!'

'We have to get him to a doctor!'

'How can we? Nearest one's miles from here in Cheyenne. He'll be dead by then.'

'The trading post!' Mercy said, brushing her bangs back. 'That's where we'll take him. Mr. McKenzie will know what to do.'

'What about Cinny? Shouldn't we be lookin' for her too?'

Mercy looked dismayed. ''Course!' she said. 'Shame on me. I was so worried about Mr. Lawless that I clean forgot about her.'

She paused and Lawless, who'd been listening to them talk with his eyes closed, now opened them and said: 'Did you find her? Was she all right?'

Mercy sadly shook her head. 'We looked everywhere, didn't we, Jonah?'

Her brother nodded miserably. His eyes were raw from lack of sleep and he looked exhausted. 'Mr. McKenzie thinks she must've gotten killed by the rockslide.'

'Says her body is still buried under all the rocks.'

'I'll never believe that,' Jonah said angrily. 'Cinny's alive. I know she is.'

Mercy smiled reassuringly at him. ''Course she is. And we'll find her, too. Can bet on that.' Turning back to

Lawless, she added: 'When the rock-slide happened, where was Cinny? Do you remember?'

Lawless searched his foggy mind. 'Right behind me, I think.'

'Behind you?' Mercy said. 'You sure about that?'

Lawless nodded. 'We were ridin' single file — '

'See!' exclaimed Jonah. 'I knew it! Cinny can't be dead 'cause the rocks . . . they were all piled in front of Mr. Lawless here.'

'What rocks?' Lawless asked, his mind beginning to clear.

'From the slide,' Mercy said. 'There was a huge pile of them blocking the way out of the canyon! Don't you remember?' she asked as he frowned.

'No.' He thought a moment; then it dawned on him. 'It must've happened after — '

'After what?'

'I got shot,' he said suddenly remembering.

'You ain't shot,' Jonah said. 'You got

hit in the head by a rock. Can ask Mrs. McKenzie if you don't believe me. She's the one who fixed you up.'

'Said you were lucky to be alive,' Mercy put in. 'Said if the rock had cut any deeper, it would've crushed your brain.'

'She may be right about my brain,' Lawless said. 'But she's wrong about it bein' a rock. It was definitely a bullet. I heard the shot.'

'But who'd want to shoot you?' Mercy asked.

'A bunch of low-life horse thieves,' Lawless said grimly, thinking: *The same pig-swillin' trash who most likely forced Cinnamon to go with them!*

13

Despite everyone's protests, Lawless insisted on dragging himself out of bed and riding to Bridger Canyon to see if he could find any proof that Cinnamon had been killed by or buried under the rockslide.

Andrew McKenzie, equally stubborn, insisted on accompanying Lawless, Mercy and Jonah. 'None of this would've happened if my boy hadnae run off with Cinnamon, so I feel obliged to help ye.'

'Jake made a mistake, I'll admit that,' Lawless said, 'but he didn't make that scum shoot me. They most likely decided that soon as I accused them of stealin' those army horses.'

'Aye, you're probably right, laddie. Nevertheless, Jake and I will go with ye. And we'll bring the mules and harness in case we need to move any of the large rocks.'

Lawless didn't argue. Nor did he mention to Mercy or Jonah that he thought Cinnamon had been abducted. Until a thorough search proved she was either dead or alive, he saw no point in adding to their misery.

On reaching the rockslide in the canyon, the five of them spread out and began looking for any trace of Cinnamon. It was hopeless. After three hours of unsuccessfully searching a wide area on both sides of the rockslide, they stopped to rest.

Lawless needed it more than the others. He felt weak and dizzy and blood had seeped through the stitches that Mrs. McKenzie had used to close the gash on his temple. Every move he made, especially bending over, made his head pound. Still he counted himself fortunate just to be alive. Whoever shot him, he realized, must have thought he was dead. And as he leaned back against a rock and felt the warmth of the sun on his face, he knew one thing for certain: If

Cinnamon *had* been abducted by those men, as he believed she had, he would never stop searching until he found her.

'Maybe it's time to use the mules,' Mercy suggested as they drank from their canteens. 'Until we look under those big rocks, I'll never believe that poor Cinny is dead.'

It took several hours to move the dozen or so boulders that were piled together in the center of the rockslide. But at last, after the mules had laboriously hauled every one of them aside and there was still no sign of Cinnamon, even Mercy was ready to accept that her sister had been killed.

Jonah wasn't. 'Just 'cause we didn't find her,' he insisted, 'don't mean she's dead. In fact, it could mean the opposite: she's still alive!'

'Then where is she?' Jake said. 'Tell me that.'

Jonah shrugged. 'I dunno. Could be anywheres. Wanderin' around lost or maybe hurt an — '

'She's not wandering around,' Lawless said, deciding not to wait anymore.

'Then where is she?' Jake repeated.

Lawless hesitated, then expelling his pain and frustration in a long weary sigh, said: 'With the bastards who shot me.'

There was a shocked silence.

'What're you saying?' Mercy said, horrified. 'They kidnapped her?'

'That's my guess,' Lawless said.

'An' it makes sense,' said Jake. Then as everyone looked at him: 'Tell 'em, Mr. Lawless. Tell 'em how they tried to force themselves on her in the store.'

Briefly, Lawless explained what happened. Mercy and Jonah grimly closed their eyes, sickened by the realization that their sister may be in the clutches of the kind of renegades Lawless had described.

'I'd sooner she was dead than that,' Mercy said.

The others remained silent, suggesting they agreed with her.

'What're we waitin' here for then?'

Jake said. 'Sooner we get started, sooner we find her.'

'Hold your horses, son,' his father said. He turned to Lawless. 'I'd dearly like to go with ye, Ben, but I have a store and a saloon to run and I cannae afford to be away for a long stretch of time — me nor my boy.'

'I understand,' Lawless said.

'But I *have* to go,' Jake began. 'Please, Pa, I — '

'Nae, lad, I'll brook no argument from ye. My mind's made up. You'll need supplies,' he added to Mercy and Jonah. 'I'll consider it a kindness if ye'll accept them from me. It's the least I can do.'

'Thank you, Mr. McKenzie,' Mercy said. 'That's most generous of you.'

'There's one other thing I can do,' McKenzie said. 'You might want to talk to this old Lakota, Shadow Wolf, who hangs around the post dancing for drinks. If it were up to me I wouldnae keep him around, but Agnes, God bless her Christian heart, has a soft spot for

114

him. To please her I let him clean out the stable for food and a wee drop of whiskey.'

'Does he speak any English?'

'Aye, but in an odd, mocking kind of fashion. Many's the time I get the feeling *he's* tolerating *me*.'

'Calls white folks citizens,' Jake said, chuckling.

'Aye, but that's nae the worst of it,' his father said. 'The man has lice and stinks worse than a wet hog.'

'Then why do I want to talk to him?' Lawless said.

'Because, laddie, he once was the finest tracker this side of the Canadian border.'

14

It was late-afternoon when they got back to the trading post. While Mercy and Jonah collected the supplies and loaded them onto one of McKenzie's mules, Lawless and Jake searched the compound for Shadow Wolf. It took a while but they eventually found him curled up behind the hog pen. He was sleeping off a drunk.

Earlier a hunting party from England had stopped at the post to replenish ammunition which had been lost on the train ride from New York. Bored, the British aristocrats had amused themselves by plying the old Lakota with whiskey so they could watch him perform Sitting Bull's infamous Ghost Dance. Shadow Wolf did not know how to dance the Ghost Dance, but he knew plenty of Lakota war dances and danced until his bare feet were bloody and he collapsed from a combination of exhaustion and too much whiskey.

Now, as Lawless kicked the Indian awake, he wondered if it was possible that this shriveled up old man with a face like a walnut, dark sad eyes and long gray braids who smelled worse than the hogs wallowing in the pen, was once a renowned tracker. But having no time to waste on finding out, he decided to take a chance that McKenzie was right. Stripping off the Lakota's filthy rags, he had Jake help him throw Shadow Wolf into a water trough. They then dressed him in a clean denim shirt and jeans bought at the store, and forced him to drink several mugs of hot black coffee until, as dusk fell, he was at last sober.

He immediately asked Lawless to buy him 'smoke.'

Lawless obliged and led Shadow Wolf to a table in the bar. Here, knowing that patience was held sacred by most Indians, he watched as the old man rolled a fat cigarette between his fingers, stuck it between his leathery lips and waited for Lawless to light it. 'Who you want me to find, citizen?' he then asked.

'What makes you think I want you to find anyone?' Lawless challenged.

Shadow Wolf stared impassively at him. 'Wisdom tells me you are not a man who pays to see an old Indian dance. Why else would you waste time on me?'

Lawless smiled. He liked this man. 'It's true,' he admitted. 'I do want you to track someone down.' He started to describe the four horse thieves. But before he was finished the old Lakota held up his wrinkly hand, stopping him. 'I know of these men,' he said. 'They come to post before, two winters ago. They promise me whiskey if I dance for them. I dance but they no pay. When I ask for my money they beat me . . . made me eat snow their horses had pissed on until I am sick. It is for this I will lead you to their cabin.'

It sounded too good to be true. 'Let

me get this straight,' Lawless said suspiciously. 'The men we speak of, the ones who made you eat bad snow, the same men who stole those six horses that were in the corral a few nights ago — you know where they are?'

'It is so, citizen.'

'This cabin; how far is it?'

'One sun, one moon.' He sucked deeply on his cigarette, held the smoke in his lungs for several moments and then expelled it with a satisfied sigh. 'Buy me whiskey and tobacco now and I will tell you the way.'

'Not a chance,' Lawless said. 'First you must lead me to them.'

'How do I know you will not cheat me as they did?'

''Cause I'll give your money to Mr. McKenzie to hold until you get back.'

'It is fair, citizen.'

'Good,' Lawless said. 'But we must leave now. These men have stolen the girl I was with and I am worried they might sell her before we find them.'

'It shall be,' Shadow Wolf said,

adding: 'This girl, she is the one with fire in her hair?'

'You saw her, then?'

'I saw her,' the Lakota said solemnly. 'And though I am old now and have no desire for a squaw's company, I am not so old that I don't understand why you want her back.'

15

It was raining lightly when the four of them left the trading post. Clouds hid the moon and stars and coyotes could be heard yip-yipping to each other in the cold, wet darkness. Led by Shadow Wolf, who was riding Jake's horse and a borrowed slicker, they rode in single file toward the distant foothills. Lawless brought up the rear, the lead rope tied to the pack-mule wrapped around his saddle horn.

After a few miles the rain stopped. Immediately, as if on cue, a wind sprang up. It blew down from the snow-tipped mountains, each icy gust making everyone appreciate their warm clothing.

Shadow Wolf rode at a steady but leisurely pace that did not suit Mercy, Jonah or Lawless. When they reached the foothills and stopped to rest the horses, his impatience spilled over. 'We're movin' too slowly,' he told the Indian. 'When we get started again, pick up the pace.'

'The horses, they will not like this.'

'So don't tell them.'

'I do not have to, citizen. They will know it by their pounding hearts.'

They mounted up and continued on into the hills. Ahead, the mountains towered high above them. Their snowy caps and white splotchy slopes reminded Lawless of an Appaloosa he once owned. Squinting up at them, he wondered how high they would have to climb. Even on a normal day he did not care for heights. They made him uneasy. How would they affect him now, with his head throbbing like a sledge hammer pounding a railroad spike?

To keep his mind from worrying about it, he thought of Cinnamon. It was a mistake. All he could visualize was her trying to fight off her kidnappers and his rage and frustration mounted.

It was then Mercy's voice jolted him back to reality. 'I have an idea,' she said to Shadow Wolf. 'What if we slept in our saddles and only ate when our horses needed rest? That would save time, wouldn't it?'

'Time is a white man's word,' the Lakota said, not looking back. 'My people have no use for it.'

Irked, Lawless said: 'How about shortcuts? Do your people have any use for one of those?'

Shadow Wolf was silent for so long, Lawless wondered if the old man had fallen asleep. 'There is such a shortcut,' he replied at last, ' — a pass that leads through the mountains.'

'Will it get us to the cabin any faster?'

'By half a day. But I must warn you, citizen, it is so narrow and dangerous even the great white goats fear to tread there.'

'I'll take my chances,' Lawless said. 'Tell me how to find it.'

'No, no, you're not going without us,' Mercy said before the old Indian could answer. 'Cinny is *our* sister, in case you have forgotten.'

'You heard the lady,' Lawless said to Shadow Wolf. 'Lead the way.'

★ ★ ★

They were in the mountains now. They rode ever upward. Each breath clouded before them. The moon came out to light their way. It was a welcome change. Suddenly everything seemed less forbidding and dangerous. Ahead, the winding dirt trail climbed between steep, rocky, tree-clad slopes that rose up on either side of them. Higher still, patches of early snow gleamed whitely in the moonlight.

As the air grew thinner the pounding in Lawless' head increased. Teeth gritted, he bore the pain in silence. No one else spoke either. The only sounds were made by the horses: labored breathing, horseshoes striking against stone.

Shortly, Shadow Wolf reined up and

raised his hand for the others to stop also.

'What now?' Lawless grumbled.

'We are almost to the pass,' the old Indian said. 'Once we enter it there can be no turning back. This is understood?'

Lawless looked at Mercy and Jonah, who nodded.

'Understood.'

Satisfied, Shadow Wolf faced front and nudged his horse forward.

Mercy, Jonah, Lawless and the pack-mule plodded after him. They rode around a blind curve, no one but the Indian knowing what to expect. Whatever it was, it wasn't what now confronted them: a short distance ahead the trail split in two. The right fork continued curving around the same mountain they were on; the left, no wider than Lawless' shoulders, angled away and entered a natural V-shaped pass that cut through an adjacent peak. A wall of sheer rock rose up on the inner side; while the outer edge dropped off for a thousand feet into a gorge.

One slip or stumble: death.

Lawless, Mercy and Jonah stared in stunned silence at the pass. Lawless felt fear for one of the rare times in his life. But he kept silent. His buckskin expressed everyone's feelings by snickering nervously and pawing at the dirt with its front hoof.

'Come, we are losing time, citizens . . . ' Shadow Wolf urged his horse on into the pass.

16

As their horses carefully picked their way along the dangerously narrow trail Lawless became aware of an eerie stillness in the pass. There was no trace of a wind. Nothing stirred. Nothing lived here. Even the few shrubs and leafless trees that protruded from the rocky slopes had long since died and now looked like shriveled claws.

To Lawless, it seemed as if God had forsaken the pass and Death and Desolation had taken over. As he rode he tried not to look down into the gorge. But now and then, as one of the horses kicked a loose stone over the edge, some strange fascination forced him to watch its freefall descent . . . as it dropped endlessly into the darkness far below.

He could not see the actual bottom of the gorge or hear the stones landing, which only added to his growing uneasiness . . . and to keep his mind occupied he began listening to the creaking of his saddle and the echoing sounds made by the hooves of the plodding horses.

He was not the only one filled with apprehension. Halfway through the pass he heard Jonah trying to whistle away his fears. But his mouth was too dry and he soon gave up. Now the only human sound came from Mercy, as she occasionally hummed softly, tunelessly to herself.

The hours dragged by. The trail climbed, dipped and twisted monotonously. Everyone seemed to lose all sense of time. They should have been tired; sleepy. But fear of falling into the gorge kept them alert.

Finally, as the overcast sky gradually began to lighten with the approach of dawn, Lawless could see the end of the pass. He judged it to be about another hundred yards. Relief surged through him. Though they still had many miles to go, at least they would be on safer ground and could rest safely for a while, maybe cook something to eat —

Suddenly, behind him, the rim of the trail broke away and stones and dirt cascaded into the gorge. The outer back leg of the normally sure-footed pack-mule slipped and went over the edge. Braying shrilly, the mule tried desperately to regain its footing. But it was a losing struggle and hindered by the weight of the packs, the panicked animal began slipping inexorably backward . . .

Lawless, feeling the lead rope jerk tautly against his saddle horn, quickly unwound it. He was just in time. As the struggling mule fell backward over the edge, the rope pulled through Lawless' gloved hands with such speed, it burned his flesh.

The hapless mule plunged into the gorge, its braying screams echoing off the sheer walls of rock.

Lawless instinctively shrank back,

away from the edge, his shoulder scraping against the side of the mountain. 'Whoa,' he said to the nervous buckskin. 'Easy, feller . . . easy . . .'

Ahead, Mercy, Jonah and Shadow Wolf stopped their horses and looked anxiously back at Lawless.

'Y-You all right, Mr. Lawless?'

For a moment he was too shaken to answer. Then getting a tight grip on his reins, he nodded and said: 'Sure . . . I'm fine. But it looks like we won't be eatin' for a spell.'

'Poor mule,' Mercy said, gazing into the gorge.

'Better mule than us,' the old Indian said unsympathetically. He faced front and kneed his horse forward.

Lawless, Mercy and Jonah followed.

And that was the end of it.

17

That afternoon they came within sight of the log cabin. Situated about a hundred feet below the trail they were on, it sat among tall stately pines in a grassy cup-shaped mountain meadow. It looked impregnable. The rear wall was protected by a rocky slope, the roof was insulated with sod and the only window was nothing but a slot wide enough to fire through — suggesting that the original owner had expected Indian attacks. Not far from the front door was a corral holding four horses, none of which belonged to Cinnamon.

'Doesn't mean your sister ain't there,' Lawless said as he saw how worried and disappointed Mercy and Jonah looked. 'Just means they most likely sold her horse.'

'Or ate it,' Shadow Wolf said solemnly.

Ignoring him, Lawless said: 'They probably got rid of it 'long with the other horses, the six they stole from the Army.'

'Makes sense,' Jonah said.

'Well, 'least we know they're in there,' Mercy said, indicating the smoke spiraling up from the chimney.

'Now all we have to do is find a way of forcing them out into the open — '

' — so we can shoot 'em!' Jonah finished.

Mercy gave her brother a withering look. 'Would that be *after* or *before* they tell us where Cinny is?'

'Knock it off, you two,' Lawless growled. 'Sniping at each other won't save your sister.' Then to the Indian: 'We'll smoke 'em out.'

Shadow Wolf nodded. 'It is what I would have done as a young warrior. But now I am too old to get onto the roof.'

'I'll do it,' Jonah said. 'Give me a few minutes to climb up on those rocks. I can jump across from there — '

'Don't jump till I tell you to,' Lawless

said. 'We got to be in position first.'

Telling Mercy and the Indian to stay behind him, he kneed the buckskin on along the trail that sloped down to the meadow.

The trail ended at a stand of Dwarf Mugo Pines. Dismounting behind the bushy dark green conifers, the three of them kept to the tree line until they were facing the cabin. They were now less than fifty yards from it. Hearts pounding in the thin air, they rested for a few moments to catch their breath; then, ducked low, they ran across the meadow and took cover behind a fallen tree. The old cedar had been felled years ago by lightning and the trunk was now overgrown by weeds and wildflowers. Crouching behind it, Lawless waited for Mercy to aim her shotgun at the cabin door and then signaled to Jonah.

Jonah waved back with his rifle and then jumped from the rocks directly behind the cabin onto the roof. The deep layer of sod dampened his landing, preventing anyone inside the cabin from hearing him. Crawling to the chimney, he pulled up two big chunks of sod. Then, holding his breath, he leaned into the smoke and stuffed the clods down the chimney. Waiting a moment to make sure that no smoke was escaping, he quickly crawled to the front edge of the roof and aimed his Winchester toward the door below.

It didn't take long. Muffled yells were heard inside the cabin. Moments later the door burst open and the four horse thieves came stumbling out, all of them coughing and rubbing their eyes.

Lawless immediately stood up and fired a warning shot at their feet. Three of the men were unarmed. But the fourth, the big man Lawless had spoken to beside the trading post corral, grabbed for his six-gun. He never cleared leather. Lawless shot him. The big man grunted, staggered back and collapsed, dead.

His three partners quickly raised their hands and the smallest, the leader, yelled: 'Don't shoot! We're unarmed!'

Lawless stepped over the dead tree and keeping the men covered, walked up to them. At the same time Jonah dropped off the cabin roof, kept his feet and aimed his rifle at their backs.

'Go get Cinnamon,' Lawless told him.

Jonah nodded and ran into the cabin.

Lawless motioned behind him. 'You can come out now,' he told Mercy and the Indian. He then confronted the leader, who was shocked to see him.

'Damn me if it ain't the Reb,' he exclaimed. 'Surely you ain't still holdin' a grudge over a few stolen broncs?'

'You got bigger trouble than stolen horses,' Lawless said grimly.

Jonah now emerged from the cabin and shook his head. 'She ain't in there.'

'Where is she?' Lawless said to the leader.

'She? She who?'

Lawless pressed his Colt against the leader's forehead. 'You got three seconds, mister. I don't see her by then, you're dead.'

'W-Wait . . . Please . . . Don't shoot . . .'
The leader backed up fearfully. 'I swear,
Reb, I don't know what you're talkin'
about.'

'My sister, Cinnamon,' Mercy said,
leveling her shotgun at him. 'She was
with Mr. Lawless when you shot him in
Bridger Canyon.'

The leader frowned, bewildered.
'Missy, you got the wrong men. Me an'
Bucky an' Wes, here, we never shot
nobody in Bridger Canyon. Hell, we
ain't even been to Bridger Canyon in
months. Have we, fellas?'

The two men shook their heads.

'Soon as we left the tradin' post,' the
one called Bucky said, 'we come
straight here.'

'Liar,' Lawless smashed him across
the face with his Colt. 'You had to stop
somewhere to sell them stolen horses.'

'No, no, he's tellin' you the truth,' the
leader said. 'We sold the horses to some
fellers drivin' beef. Theirs was all wore
out.'

'Like my patience,' Lawless said.

'Now, for the last time, where's the girl?'

'Tell him, citizen,' Shadow Wolf urged. 'Else he *will* kill you.'

'Can't tell him what I don't know,' the leader whined. Then to Lawless: 'Be reasonable, Reb. We'd be crazy to steal that girl. Hair that color, hell, wouldn't be no time atall 'fore somebody seen her. She'd be nothin' but trouble for us.'

''Sides, if we wanna bed a woman,' put in Bucky, 'there's plenty of whores and squaws just for the askin'.'

'They're lyin',' Jonah said to Lawless. 'Can't you see that?'

Lawless began counting. 'One . . . two . . . '

'For chrissake,' the leader whimpered. 'Why won't you believe us? Can't you see we're tellin' you the truth?'

'Three.'

Lawless shot him.

The leader screamed, clutched his bleeding thigh and collapsed.

'Last chance,' Lawless said, aiming his gun at the leader's head. 'Next one's in your brain.'

'You kill him,' Bucky warned, 'it'll be straight up murder.'

Lawless smiled mirthlessly. 'If you're hopin' I got a conscience, friend, you're beatin' the wrong mule.' He started to squeeze the trigger.

'No! ' Mercy stepped in front of him. 'He's right. It is murder.'

'You sayin' you believe this dirt?'

'Yes. And that's the truth of it.'

'Well, you can believe all you want,' Jonah said angrily, 'not me. If you ain't gonna shoot 'em, Mr. Lawless, I will.'

'You'll do no such thing, Jonah Kincannon! Now put that rifle down and get some sense in that thick head of yours. I want to find Cinny as much as anyone,' Mercy added to Lawless. 'But not by murdering the wrong men.'

'Just 'cause your sister ain't here,' he replied, 'don't mean they don't know where she is. They could've sold her a dozen places 'fore comin' here.'

'But we didn't,' Bucky said emphatically. 'We didn't shoot you. We didn't steal no girl. An' we didn't sell nobody to nobody. An' that's Gospel, mister!'

Lawless chewed on the denial. To have killed one of these four men for the wrong reason did not bother him. They were horse thieves and that alone, he felt, was reason enough to shoot them. But to now have to admit that they hadn't kidnapped Cinnamon meant also admitting that he had no idea where she was, or who had taken her — or even if she was still alive — and that was almost more than he could swallow. His disappointment was overwhelming.

He took a deep breath and let it all out in a long weary sigh. He looked at the dead man, at the leader bleeding on the ground, at the Colt in his hand. Then holstering the gun, he said to Bucky: 'Take him inside an' see to his leg. You go with 'em,' he told Jonah. 'Make sure they don't get an itch for their guns.'

'I'll go with him,' Mercy said. 'See what's on the stove.'

Lawless waited until he was alone with the Indian. 'Go get the horses, old man. Soon as we've eaten an' rested some, we'll be headin' back.'

'Long way or through pass?'

'Long way,' Lawless said. 'I've had my fill of shortcuts.'

Shadow Wolf smiled. He started away then stopped and looked back at Lawless. 'My people have a saying: 'A man with no conscience is like a river with no water. Both soon dry up and turn to dust.'

Lawless spat his feelings into the grass. 'My people have a saying too,' he said. 'Never sober up a drunken Indian. He makes no sense.' Stepping over the corpse, he headed for the cabin.

18

The next morning, after a breakfast of beans and leftover venison stew, the four of them started back down the mountain. They left the three horse thieves in the cabin, Lawless warning them that if it turned out they were lying and knew where Cinnamon was, he would hunt them down and kill them.

The wide scenic trail that descended toward the foothills was steep and winding, but not dangerous. With Shadow Wolf leading the way, they rode in silence through mountain passes, verdant valleys and canyons whose rocky slopes were home to herds of wild white goats; past mirror-surfaced lakes that reflected the tree-lined shores and the clear blue sky, and eventually across meadows afire with blooming shrubs and shallow streams that teemed with trout.

At noon they stopped beside a fast-moving creek to give the weary horses a blow. Lawless, Mercy and Jonah were equally grateful for the rest. Only the Indian seemed tireless. After quenching his thirst in the cold clear water, he walked in a circle several times then picked up a handful of white stones, carefully chose one and threw it into the creek.

'Look at that old man,' Lawless grumbled. 'Looks as fresh as when we started.'

'Maybe he ain't as old as he looks,' Jonah said.

'Isn't, not ain't,' his sister corrected.

Jonah ignored her and watched as Shadow Wolf now sat cross-legged on the grass facing the mountain they had just left, closed his eyes and began to chant.

'Now what's he doin' — prayin'?'

'Looks like,' Lawless said. 'Probably thankin' the mountain for not killin' us.'

'Can't say it didn't try,' Jonah said.

'Just ask Mr. McKenzie's mule.'

'We're must pay him back somehow,' Mercy said, brushing her bangs aside. 'Maybe give him one of our horses or two of our goats.'

'I ain't givin' him my horse,' Jonah said. 'Not for no jug-eared mule.'

His sister glared at him. 'Are you deliberately tryin' to strain my patience?'

Jonah grinned at her. 'Sorry. I 'isn't' giving him my horse. There — that make you feel better?' Before she could reply, he added to Lawless: 'You thought of anybody else yet who might have shot you?'

'Uh-uh. But it's a long list.'

They fell silent, each thinking of Cinnamon in their own way. High overhead an eagle screamed. They looked up and watched as the great golden brown bird floated lazily on the thermals.

'Wish I could fly,' Mercy said. 'Looks so quiet and peaceful up there.'

'Problem is,' Lawless continued, as if he hadn't stopped talking, 'no one on that list has any reason for kidnappin' Cinnamon.'

'Which means,' Jonah said glumly, 'we got as much chance of findin' her as flyin' like that eagle.'

A shadow leaned over them. They looked up and saw Shadow Wolf standing in front of them. 'I need tobacco, citizen,' he said solemnly to Lawless.

Lawless dug his tobacco pouch out of his shirt pocket and gave it to the Indian. 'Help yourself, amigo.' He dug out cigarette papers, adding: 'Here.'

Shadow Wolf shook his head, 'Not need,' turned and walked over to a flat rock beside the creek. Shading his eyes with his hand, he looked up at the eagle, now a tiny speck in the sky. He spoke silently to it for a moment; then he spilled tobacco out of the pouch onto the rock, looked up at the eagle again then returned beside Lawless and gave him the almost-empty pouch.

'What the hell . . . ?' began Lawless.

'Patience,' Shadow Wolf said. He

went and sat beside the creek, closed his eyes and began to chant softly.

'Serves me right,' Lawless grumbled. 'I should know better than to treat an Indian like a white man — '

'Look!' Mercy said, pointing.

Her brother and Lawless followed her finger as it pointed at the eagle. The huge bird was diving straight toward them. They watched, open-mouthed, as the eagle came plummeting earthward then at the last instant, when a collision seemed inevitable, the bird opened its wings and gracefully glided toward the rock. It landed on it, stared unblinkingly at Lawless, Mercy and Jonah — then scooped up the tobacco with its beak and launched itself into the air. The flapping of its outspread wings caused a draft that touched their faces as the eagle flew upward, gradually gaining altitude, until it was lost in the blue heavens.

'Did you see that?' Jonah said, awed. 'My God, *did you see that?*'

Neither Lawless nor Mercy answered

him. They were still trying to grasp what had just happened.

The Indian returned and stood before them. 'It is done,' he said.

'What's done?' Jonah said.

'The eagle spoke to me. I must help you find the girl with fire in her hair.'

'An' just how the hell you figure on doin' that?' Lawless asked. 'By throwin' another stone in the water?'

Shadow Wolf tapped the pouch hanging around his waist. 'I am to ask the Four Directions to guide us.'

'Four Directions?' Lawless echoed. 'What the hell's the — ?'

Mercy cut him off. 'Do what you must,' she told the Indian. Then to Lawless and her brother: 'At this point, I'm willing to try anything to get Cinny back, even Indian hocus-pocus.'

19

By the time they reached the hills it was too dark to continue. They made camp in a small canyon, sheltered by a pile of rocks shaped by timeless winds. It was not as numbingly cold as in the mountains, but cold enough to make them keep their coats on. The mournful howl of wolves echoed in the night air, making the horses uneasy and skittish.

Lawless gave instructions that they were to be kept close to camp. While he and Jonah unsaddled the horses and fastened the hobbies, Mercy shot a rabbit, skinned it and cooked it on a stick over a fire made by the old Indian.

'It isn't much,' she apologized as they sat around the fire to eat, 'not for four starving people, but at least we won't go to bed hungry.'

'Wouldn't be the first time,' her brother grumbled.

'Jonah Kincannon, shame on you! That is not true!' Mercy looked at Lawless and the old Lakota. 'We may not always have had food aplenty, I'll admit, but never once has the table been bare. And that's the truth of it.'

'No shame in goin' hungry,' Lawless said. 'Happened to me many times over the years. An' I'm sure it's happened to you, too,' he said to Shadow Wolf.

'Without the buffalo,' the Indian said sadly, 'it has become a way of life for my people. It is the same for the Cheyenne, Crow, Arapaho and many other tribes. All of us who fought the Long Knives have had to learn to live with empty bellies and the pain of watching our elderly and our children starve to death.'

'Well, I think it's terrible,' Mercy said, 'terrible and unfair. And no matter what it takes, I intend to see that it never happens to us. You and your brother and sister,' she added to Jonah, 'will never go hungry. Not so long as I'm in charge of this family!'

'It may not be your call,' Jonah said glumly. 'Not if we don't find Cinny.'

'We *will* find her. That I promise you!' Mercy turned to Lawless for confirmation. 'Won't we, Ben?'

'Count on it,' he said. As he spoke he took out his tobacco pouch and papers intending to roll a smoke. But there wasn't enough tobacco left for even one cigarette. Irked, he scowled at the old Indian. 'That eagle better be right 'bout the Four Directions, 'cause I get awful salty when I don't have me a smoke.'

'Patience,' Shadow Wolf said solemnly. 'Eagles do not lie.'

★ ★ ★

Jonah woke in the middle of the night. He was not sure why — until he heard the soft chanting of the old Lakota. Shivering, he sat up, pulled the blanket tightly around him and looked across the glowing embers of the fire and saw the Indian sitting, cross-legged and bare-chested, with his arms held up to the sky.

Fascinated, Jonah continued watching. Shortly Shadow Wolf stopped chanting, lowered his arms and took something from his waist-pouch. His body blocked what it was and Jonah had to lean to his left in order to see it.

It was a small, rawhide-bound, wooden medicine wheel with an equilateral cross attached to the underside. Each arm of the cross was a different color — red, yellow, black, or white — as were the matching four quarters of the wheel. The soft white downy feathers of a baby eagle decorated a dangling strip of rawhide.

Shadow Wolf now placed the wheel on the ground and shifted positions so that his back was to the north. Leaning over the South-facing quarter of the wheel as if he were entering it, he began to chant again. Over a period of an hour or so he shifted positions three more times, next 'entering' the West; then the North; and lastly the East.

When he was finished, he sat motionless for several minutes in silent prayer. Then, returning the medicine wheel to his pouch, he rose and looked impassively at Jonah as if he had known all along the youth was watching him.

'Wake your sister and the man called Lawless. When I return I will tell them of what I have learned.'

'You goin' somewhere?' Jonah said as the Indian started away.

Shadow Wolf ignored him and walked off into the darkness.

★   ★   ★

It was almost dawn by the time the old Lakota returned to camp. By then the fire was blazing and Lawless, Mercy and Jonah were fully dressed and Lawless was grumbling about the lack of tobacco and hot coffee.

'This better be good,' he warned Shadow Wolf. 'Thanks to you feedin' that damn eagle my tobacco, I'm feelin' mighty testy.'

'Hush,' Mercy told him. Then to the Indian: 'Why were you gone so long?'

When Shadow Wolf did not reply right away Jonah said to his sister: 'See, sis, what'd I tell you? He ain't talkin' to no one.'

For once Mercy didn't bother to correct him. 'Does it have something to do with the Four Directions?'

The old Lakota sat wearily beside the fire. He looked drained.

'I could not answer you before,' he said to Jonah, 'because I was in a holy state. I should not have even spoken the few words I did. In this state,' he added, now including Lawless and Mercy, 'I must not speak or be touched. If this happens I risk angering the god of the earth.'

'I'm sorry,' Jonah said. 'I didn't know.'

Unimpressed, Lawless said: 'So what did you learn, old man — if anythin'?'

'Did your god tell you where my sister is,' Mercy blurted, 'or who took her?'

'I see many things,' Shadow Wolf said imperiously. 'I see Purity, Family, Innocence, an Amazement of Life . . . I see Youth, Friendship, Manhood, Solitude and an Inner Peace — all things the Earth must have in order to find balance — '

'Forget the Council Fire lingo,' Lawless broke in irritably. 'Cut to the meat. Did you find out where Cinnamon is?'

'The Four Directions must be in balance,' Shadow Wolf continued, unfazed by Lawless' outburst, 'for all to be well with the world.'

'Jesus,' began Lawless, then fell silent as Mercy glared at him.

'Just as a family must have balance. Yours once did,' the Indian said to Mercy. 'Four children: two male, two female, father and mother. Now it doesn't. And without this balance, without your sister — '

'You gonna answer my question?' Lawless demanded. 'Or am I gonna hold your goddamn head in that fire?'

'Mr. Lawless,' Mercy snapped. 'Control yourself. Go on, please,' she told the Indian.

Shadow Wolf looked directly at Lawless. 'Men with hair have taken this girl you seek.'

'That's it?' Lawless exclaimed. 'That's all you got to tell me? After all this chantin' and prayin' Jonah here says you done — after disappearin' for hours 'cause you don't want folks to talk to you or touch you — the best you can come up with is 'men with hair' have snatched Cinnamon? Judas Priest, you old fake, I oughta shoot you right where you goddamn stand!'

Unperturbed, Shadow Wolf said calmly: 'The hair that these men have hangs from their saddles.'

For one infinitesimal moment it didn't register with Lawless, Mercy or Jonah.

Then Lawless, almost in a whisper, said: 'Scalp hunters!'

20

'It makes sense,' Lawless said when everyone had calmed down. 'Scum like that, hell, they'd kidnap an' sell their own kin if it brought a profit.'

'But they never saw Cinny,' Mercy reminded. 'She was still hiding in the cabin with me when they rode off.'

'Wrong,' Lawless said. 'While they were waterin' their horses, she peered out the window. I saw her. The old man saw her. He even mentioned it in a sort round-about way. Said somethin' about it was nice to have a woman to warm your feet on at night. I didn't catch on at the time, but — '

'She *did* look out,' Jonah said to his sister. 'I told her not to but you know Cinny — always does the opposite of what you tell her.'

'Also,' Lawless added, 'they rode off toward the trading post.'

'Which means they had to go through Bridger Canyon — '

'Maybe they came back that way too,' Lawless said grimly. 'That would account for why they were there when Cinnamon an' me rode through — '

'Bush-whackin' bastards,' said Jonah.

'I've told you not to use that word,' Mercy scolded.

'Aw, sis, stop treatin' me like I'm twelve years old.'

'When you stop acting like it, I will,' she said. Then to Lawless: 'I'm not saying the scalpers didn't do what you said. I'm just trying to make sense out of it. I mean, why would they go in one direction then double back the way they came, unless they had a logical reason?'

Lawless thought a moment before saying: 'Maybe they needed food or supplies to carry them through the winter?'

'Or 'cause they were going some-where,' put in Jonah.

'That's easy enough to prove,' Mercy said. 'We can describe them to Jake and his Pa and ask if they remember seeing them that day or the next.'

'Mr. McKenzie might even know them,' Jonah said. 'This most likely ain't the first time they've stopped there — '

'It is not,' Shadow Wolf said quietly. 'It is one of many times.'

'You've seen 'em there?' Lawless said.

'I have seen them.'

'Would know 'em if you saw them again?'

'I would know them,' the old Indian said.

'Even though most of the time you were piss-drunk?'

Shadow Wolf stared impassively at him. 'Do you have kin, citizen?'

'A cousin. Will.'

'Would you remember men who rode with his scalp on their saddle?'

'Jesus. One of those scalps was your brother's?'

'No. But two of them were lifted from old men who rode alongside me when we fought the Long Knives. We Lakotas have long memories. I will

157

never forget these men.'

'Did you ever hear the scalpers talk about where they lived or might be going?' Mercy asked. 'When they were drinking in the saloon, I mean?'

Shadow Wolf shook his head.

'The Southwest!' Lawless said as it dawned on him. Then as the others looked at him in surprise: 'We were talkin', the old man an' me, 'bout how cold it was in Wyoming. Said he was tired of winterin' here. I said my cousin felt the same way, that's why he stayed in Texas. I don't remember his exact words, but when he was leavin' the old man said if he didn't ride south to warmer climes, he might see me again someday.'

'You think they took Cinny to Texas?' Jonah said, alarmed.

Lawless shrugged. 'It's a long shot, I know. But right now it's all we got.'

'B-But that's hundreds, maybe thousands of miles from here! We'll *never* find her!' Suddenly, tears bubbled from his eyes.

'Never's a big word,' Lawless said gently. 'Hell, few minutes ago we didn't even know *who* kidnapped Cinnamon. Now, thanks to Shadow Wolf here, we not only have a fair idea, but might even know where they took her. That's better'n nothin', ain't it?'

'R-Reckon so,' Jonah said, sniffing back his tears.

'You bet it is,' Mercy said. Brushing her bangs back, she put her arm fondly about his shoulders. 'Don't worry, Jonah. We'll find Cinny. I know we will.' She led him away.

Lawless offered his hand to Shadow Wolf. 'Reckon I owe you an apology.'

'Not me, citizen,' the old Lakota said. 'It is the eagle you cast doubt upon.'

'Well, next time you an' the big fella have a powwow,' Lawless said wryly, 'be sure to pass along how sorry I am.'

21

'Aye, I know them well,' Andrew McKenzie said. He paused to wipe the sweat from his brow then nodded for his son, Jake to finish unloading the freight wagon and led Lawless, Mercy, Jonah and Shadow Wolf into the general store. 'Mind ye, Jules Blackthorn and his brood of no-goods are nae the kind of clientele I like to do business with, but money's money, 'specially in these hard times.'

'When's the last time you saw them?' Lawless said.

'I can tell ye exactly,' the Scotsman said. He went behind the counter and thumbed through the pages of his business ledger. 'Let me see . . . uhm . . . aye, here it be — Blackthorn.' He turned the ledger around so that it faced Lawless and the others, and pointed at an entry. 'Twelve days ago.'

'*Twelve days?*' Jonah looked at his sister in dismay. 'They could be halfway to Texas by now!'

'Calm down,' Lawless soothed. 'We don't even know if they're headed for Texas. They didn't happen to say where they were goin',' he added to McKenzie, 'did they?'

'Not to me, laddie, no. But then Jules knows I dinnae care for their company, so he wouldnae be likely to share his thoughts with me.'

'Maybe they said somethin' to Jake,' Jonah said. 'Or maybe he overheard them talkin' or somethin'.'

'Aye, could be,' McKenzie said. 'That boy of mine, he can chin-wag with the best of them.' He went to the door and called to his son. Moments later Jake entered, hair plastered to his forehead, shirt dark with sweat. 'Yeah, Pa?'

'When the Blackthorns were here last, did they happen to mention where they were off to?'

'California.'

161

'California?' Mercy looked at Lawless, who shrugged.

'No,' Jake corrected, 'Weren't California, 'twas Colorado.'

'You sure 'bout that?' Lawless said.

'Aye. Mr. Blackthorn's horse had thrown a shoe and he asked me to have the blacksmith replace it. Then he changed his mind and told me get all the shoes replaced. Said they were going to Colorado to see his brother who'd struck silver and didnae want to risk losing another shoe in the mountains.' Jake paused, screwed his face into a frown and scratched his head before adding: 'One of his sons, Lucas, I think it was, then joked 'bout how after that they were going someplace hot where his Pa's bones didnae freeze.'

'Texas, most likely,' Lawless said, thinking aloud.

There was silence save for a fly buzzing against the window. As if on cue, McKenzie grabbed a fly swatter, went to the window and mashed the fly. He then scooped it up with the swatter, returned behind the counter and dropped the dead fly into a waste basket. ''Tis not my nature to kill wee beasties,' he said as if needing to explain his actions, 'but flies now . . . I consider them an exception.'

'You figure that's where they've taken Cinny?' Jake asked Lawless.

'Possible.'

'You going after them?'

'Yeah.'

'Wish I could go with you,' Jake said, avoiding his father's glare. 'But since I can't, when you do find Cinny I'd be obliged if you'd let me know.'

'Got my word on it,' Lawless promised.

'Get back to work now, lad,' McKenzie told his son. 'Those crates willnae unload themselves.'

Jake rolled his eyes at Lawless, Mercy and Jonah and hurried out.

'Mr. McKenzie,' Mercy said, 'I have a favor to ask you?'

'If it be about supplies, Miss Kincannon, ye dinnae have to worry about — '

'Please, let me finish,' she said. Then as the Scotsman subsided: 'I have no idea how long it's going to take my brothers and me to find our sister, or how far we'll have to go. But I can say with certainty that no matter how long it takes, all of us will keep looking until we *do* find her.'

'That goes for me, too,' Lawless said quietly.

Mercy and Jonah exchanged smiles of relief.

'I can't tell you how much we appreciate that,' Mercy said. ''Fraid we've come to rely on you more than we should.'

'An' you can continue doin' so, got my word on that. But I want to warn you both,' Lawless said. 'Less we get a run of luck, it ain't gonna be easy to track the Blackthorns down. Considerin' how much territory we got to cover, be like lookin' for a mouse in a haystack.'

'I will find your mouse,' Shadow Wolf said. He had not spoken since they had

164

entered the storeroom and for most of the conversation, had been looking at the bottles of whiskey in the display case as if trying to 'will' them into his hands. But now he stood as tall and straight as his old bones would allow, and spoke with the authority of a veteran tracker. 'And I will not ask for money to do so.'

Lawless and the others looked at the old Lakota in surprise.

'Why would you want to do that?' Jonah asked suspiciously. 'She ain't your sister.'

'Mind your tongue,' Mercy snapped. Then politely to the Indian: 'It is very kind of you to offer, Shadow Wolf, but we could be gone a long time and the journey could be very hard — '

'This I already know.'

'And you still want to go?'

'I must go,' Shadow Wolf said simply. 'It is written.'

'Then we'll be happy to have you,' Mercy said. 'Won't we, Mr. Lawless?'

'Dee-lighted,' he said straight-faced.

Then to the old Indian: 'Reckon I'll have to lay in a store of tobacco 'case you'n that eagle get to powwowin' again.'

'Don't worry,' Mercy said. 'That will be included in our supplies. Now, sir,' she said to McKenzie, 'to business. I have decided, and I'm sure my brothers will agree, that in order to pay for everything we buy from you, I will write you an IOU and leave you the deed to our land and everything on it as — '

'Whoa, hold your horses,' Lawless said. 'You can't do that. You and your brothers won't have nothin' to return to if we find your sister.'

'*When* we find her,' Mercy corrected, adding: 'I'm well aware of that, Mr. Lawless, but the Kincannons do not accept charity. That was instilled in me very early in my childhood, and — '

'Tell you what I will do, lass,' McKenzie cut in. 'I'll take ye deed, but I'll nae register it in my name. I'll keep it locked in the safe and merely consider it as collateral. That way, if

— *when* — ye find Miss Cinnamon and return, the lands will still be yours — '

'But we'll be broke,' Mercy said.

'Dinnae worry,' McKenzie said. 'I'm sure we can work out some kind of acceptable arrangement. Now,' he added before she could protest, 'I have chores to do. So make up a list of what ye'll need, and I'll have Jake get everything for ye.'

'We're also gonna need another pack-mule,' Lawless said as the Scotsman started to leave the store. 'The one you loaned us lost its footin' an' fell into a gorge.'

'But we intend to pay you for it,' Mercy said quickly. 'You can add it to the price of supplies.'

'Dinnae worry, lass,' McKenzie said. 'I'll keep a fair tally on everything. By the by,' he added to Lawless. 'I take it then ye never found the men with the stolen horses?'

'We found 'em,' Lawless said. 'But they weren't the ones who kidnapped Cinnamon.'

★ ★ ★

Right before they left, Shadow Wolf insisted on talking to the blacksmith. When Lawless demanded to know why, the old Lakota said simply: 'Important.'

'Then we will all go,' Mercy said firmly.

'Aw, for chrissake,' Lawless said. But by the stubborn look in her large brown eyes he knew he was spitting in the wind and, grumbling, he agreed.

The blacksmith shop was behind the livery stable. It was a lean-to, with no walls except for the rear wall of the stable and tarpaulin thrown over a trellis of two-by-fours for a roof. But it suited the blacksmith or farrier, as Karl Siegfried preferred to be called. A short powerful German who spoke very little English, he was busy shoeing a freight-wagon horse when Lawless and the Kincannons reined up outside his shop. He glanced up briefly, but his scowl as he saw Shadow Wolf dismounting told the

168

Indian he wasn't welcome.

'*Kommen Sie von mir, Sie alt betrunken weg!*'

Unfazed, Shadow Wolf said with great dignity: 'I am not drunk. And I will not go till I see a new shoe.'

The farrier, accustomed to the old Indian stumbling away when berated, hammered home the last nail, lowered the horse's leg and said: 'Vot for you vant to see zer new shoe?'

'Show me and I tell you.'

'Show the man,' Lawless said from his saddle. 'Could be important.'

Grudgingly, the farrier took a new shoe from a rack of new shoes and threw it to Shadow Wolf.

The old Lakota examined it thoroughly. 'This same kind of shoe you put on Mr. Blackthorn's horse?'

'Yah.'

Shadow Wolf nodded, solemnly, tossed the shoe back to the farrier and mounted his horse. 'We go now,' he told Lawless.

'Hey,' the farrier yelled as the old Lakota wheeled his horse around. 'You not say for why you vant to see zer new shoe.'

'I forget,' Shadow Wolf lied. He rode off. The others followed him.

No one spoke again until they had ridden out of the trading post. Then when they were a short distance on along the trail leading southwest, Lawless reined up and turned to the Indian. 'All right, let's have it. Why'd you want to look at that shoe?'

'When I am young,' the old Lakota said, 'I ride with warriors to Colorado to get back ponies stolen by the Utes.'

'I'm impressed,' Lawless said. 'So, what?'

'Much mountain there. Our ponies not wear shoes. They slip and fall. Many lose lives.'

'So?'

'Wait,' Mercy said. 'I think I know what he's trying to say.' To Shadow Wolf, she said: 'If Mr. Blackthorn and his sons did go to Colorado, like Jake said, their horses are shod and will not fall. Right, Shadow Wolf?'

'Yes, but not ordinary shoe. Special shoe to get more grip.' He shaped his hand like a horseshoe and indicated the heel and toe, saying: 'Add more metal here and here.'

'He means caulks or mud-studs,' Lawless said. 'An' because of the caulks, you can track Blackthorn's horse, that it?'

The old Lakota beamed. 'You are not so stupid, citizen.'

'That's great! ' Jonah said. 'Means we got a chance of findin' them.'

'Yeah, but what if other horses have the same kind of shoes?' Mercy said. 'How will you know the difference?'

'*Herr* Siegfried very proud man. Want everyone to know his shoes. Stamp letters KS on them.' With a smug smile, the old Lakota rode on.

Mercy looked happily at Lawless. 'He is so-o smart. Aren't you glad you agreed to let him come with us?'

'Reckon,' Lawless said. 'But he gets on my nerves.'

★ ★ ★

That night, wanting to keep the horses fresh for the long journey, they camped in a ravine, sheltered from the wind by a stand of junipers. Everyone was exhausted, but none of them could silence their thoughts and concerns about Cinnamon and sleep did not come easily.

Lawless and Shadow Wolf remained smoking at the fire long after the Kincannons were snuggled in their blankets. Keeping his voice low, Lawless spoke looking into the dying flames.

''Bout those horseshoes,' he said grudgingly. 'That was smart thinkin'.'

'Came at steep price,' the old Lakota replied. 'I lose only brother when we fight Utes. Not think much about him till now. Sadness not good.'

Lawless studied the Indian across the fire. 'You're a puzzle, old man.'

'Not understand.'

'Sure you do. You're one smart

172

Indian. You know it. I'm gettin' to know it. So quit tryin' to pretend you ain't.'

Shadow Wolf thought a moment. 'It is agreed then,' he said solemnly. 'We both know I am smart. What is your point, citizen?'

'My goddamn point,' Lawless said, irked, 'is why do you sometimes talk like a feller with schoolin' an' other times in pidgin English?'

The old Lakota locked gazes with him. It might have been the reflection of the dancing flames, but Lawless was sure he saw a twinkle in them.

'Knowing you are smart is the first step to arrogance and arrogance leads to downfall,' Shadow Wolf said stoically. 'Sometimes I need to remind myself how far my people have fallen.'

22

It was barely daylight when Mercy closed the door of the Kincannon cabin. Stepping off the porch, she started toward her brothers who stood nearby with Lawless and Shadow Wolf. But after a few steps she paused, turned, brushed back her bangs, and looked at the cabin for what she hoped was not the last time. Her eyes stung. She realized she was crying and quickly wiped the tears away.

'I know it's foolish,' she said as she joined the others, 'but I'm really going to miss our little home.'

'Understandable,' Lawless said. 'Every time you get attached to a place an' then have to move on, you leave a little piece of yourself behind.'

'What a lovely way of putting it,' she said. 'And so true. But who knows,' she added cheerfully, 'could be we'll be back 'fore you know it.'

'*With Cinny*,' Caleb said. He looked older and thinner, suggesting being alone didn't agree with him. 'That's the important thing to remember.'

'Think the goats will be all right while we're gone?' Jonah said.

'Sure, they'll do just fine,' Mercy said. 'Same as the chickens. They get hungry enough they'll soon start scrounging around. Now, can we go?' she asked, mounting up beside Lawless. 'If I stay here much longer, I'm going to bawl my eyes out. And that's the truth of it.'

They left.

As they rode across the prairie toward the Colorado border, Shadow Wolf glanced upward . . . wondering as he did if the almost invisible black speck circling high above them was the same eagle . . .

*   *   *

The Colorado border was only fifteen miles from the cabin. The weather was cool and overcast, but the threat of rain held off. Despite the plodding, heavily-laden pack-mule, they made good time and it was still afternoon when they crossed the line. There was little change in the scenery ahead: vast open grassland dotted with silvery-green sagebrush stretching toward the vague, bluish outlines of distant mountains.

So far they had not seen any hoof-prints with caulks or Karl Siegfried's initials, but neither had they really expected to. The trail was well-used by riders and freight wagons, the big heavy wheels of the latter crushing everything they rolled over into dust.

They rode until dusk then camped in a sheltered gully on the outskirts of Sagebrush. Leaving Shadow Wolf to start a fire and Mercy and her brothers to take care of the horses, Lawless rode into town to make inquiries about the Blackthorns.

Sagebrush wasn't much to look at, just a row of false-front buildings lining the old Overland Trail with a few dirt side-streets leading back to scattered cabins. Change the name, Lawless thought as he rode past a barbershop, saloon, church and feed and grain store, and it could be any of a hundred other little towns he'd ridden through in Texas and New Mexico.

Reining up outside Parker's Livery Stable, he nodded politely to an old man sucking on a pipe by the open doors. 'Evenin', mister.'

'Evenin', son. Got me a clean stall if you're figurin' on overnightin' that buckskin.'

'Thanks. But I'm tryin' to catch up to some kin of mine. Maybe you saw them or grained their horses — my uncle an' four cousins, name of Blackthorn. Come to mind, do you?'

The old man shook his head. 'Uh-uh.' Turning his pipe upside down he tapped it on his gnarled palm, emptying the bowl, and then blew into the stem to get rid of any loose tobacco. ''Course now, I ain't sayin' they didn't ride through, mind. But they sure never give me the time of day.'

''Obliged.'

Lawless tipped his hat and nudged his horse forward. Ahead, several miners were laughing outside a saloon built of unpainted lumber. Lawless reined up and asked them the same question he'd asked the old man. Getting the same answer, he wheeled his horse around and rode back to camp.

It thundered during the night. Crawling out of their blankets they barely had time to grab their slickers before the rain came. It lashed them with savage fury for ten minutes or so, causing rivulets of mud to swirl around their ankles, and then stopped as abruptly as it had started.

'Not good for finding tracks,' Shadow Wolf said, eyeing the rain-sodden ground.

'Or for blankets,' Mercy said ruefully. She picked hers up, water dripping from it, and started to wring it out.

Nearby, her brothers did the same to theirs.

'Let's hope we don't have to cross any rivers,' Lawless said. 'Rain like this can turn 'em into white water.'

Caleb muttered something under his breath.

'What did you say?' Mercy asked him.

'Nothin'.'

'Yes you did. Tell me.'

When Caleb refused to answer, Jonah grabbed him in a headlock. 'Tell her,' he said as his younger brother struggled to break loose. 'Tell her or I'll twist your head off.'

'Stop it!' Mercy told him. 'Let him go!'

Grudgingly, Jonah obeyed. Caleb immediately punched him on the cheek, staggering him. A moment later the brothers were grappling in the mud.

Mercy eyed them with disgust then said to Lawless: 'This is a mean thing to say, but sometimes they're more trouble than they're worth.'

'Shoot them,' Shadow Wolf said solemnly. 'More food for us.'

Lawless chuckled despite himself. Bending over the two boys, he grabbed each one by the hair and dragged them apart. He then buried their faces in the mud, holding them down until they were spluttering for air. Finally releasing them, he hunkered down before them and wagged his finger in their muddy faces.

'I ain't your father,' he warned, 'but if you two don't quit fightin' an' start shoulderin' some responsibility, I swear I'll beat the pants off you.'

'Don't look at me,' Mercy said as her brothers turned to her. 'Like Ben says, it's time you grew up, both of you.'

'Wasn't my fault,' Jonah grumbled. 'If Caleb, here, had told you what he said none of this would've happened.'

'I was gonna tell her,' his brother said, 'but you started stranglin' me.'

'So tell her now.'

'You don't have to if you don't want to,' Mercy said. 'Not that important.'

Caleb's lower lip trembled and for a moment it looked as if he might cry. Then, voice full of emotion, he said: 'It's Cinny . . . '

'What about her?' Lawless said when Caleb stopped.

'What you said 'bout the rain an' the whitewater . . . she can't swim, Mr. Lawless.'

23

They broke camp at sunup the next morning. Bellies full of beans, bacon and biscuits they rode on through Sagebrush and followed the trail as it continued to wind through the low brown hills toward the high country.

The rain had washed the air clean. It smelled fresh and piney and was so dry in the bright cold sunlight that it seemed to crackle in their ears. Though the climb was gradual it was steady and by mid-day, with the air thinner now and breathing more difficult, they were more than seven thousand feet above sea level and had reached the Yampa River.

Here, along the banks, it was grassy and lined with bushes while across the river the nearby foothills were dark with coniferous forests that climbed up the lower slopes of the Rocky Mountains.

They rode on, following the ever-winding river whenever possible. For the most part it was wide and in places shallow enough to cross. Today, due to last night's rain, there were signs indicating that the water had briefly overflowed its banks and then retreated, leaving the ground muddy. Already riders and wagons had crossed at several of these places and at each one Shadow Wolf dismounted and carefully examined all the hoof-prints.

Lawless and the others watched him from their saddles. It seemed to take forever and everyone but the Indian grew impatient. But no amount of urging could hurry the old man. He was an Indian who trusted his instincts and his instincts told him to study everything meticulously before making a decision. At last, when they had stopped for a third time and he had examined all the prints, he saw something that made him kneel and peer closely at the ground.

'What is it?' Lawless called to him.

'Two prints.'

Dismounting, Lawless handed his reins to Mercy and approached the old Lakota. 'With caulks?'

'Yes.' The Indian looked up, expressionless. 'But no letters KS.'

Lawless kneeled beside the Indian, 'Show me,' and looked at the ground where Shadow Wolf indicated. Two hoof-prints showed in the trampled mud. Both had caulk marks front and back, but no trace of any initials.

Straightening up, Lawless looked about him. As far as he could see the mud had been churned up by wagon wheels and other horses whose shoes did not have caulks.

'Is it them?' Mercy asked hopefully.

Lawless shrugged. 'Most likely not,' he said. Then to the Indian: 'Could the initials have been there but gotten filled up with mud?'

Shadow Wolf shook his head. 'Letters stamped here,' he said, pointing to the left of the indentation made by the front caulk. 'If mud destroy letters, it

184

destroy print too.'

They rode on. Though they stopped at several other places where riders had forded the river, the old Indian could find no trace of caulk marks. The continual disappointment began to wear down the Kincannon brothers. They began arguing, disagreeing over senseless things, like how high they had climbed, whose horse was more tired, or who should be riding ahead of whom — until finally their constant bickering got on Mercy's nerves and she yelled at them to shut up.

'One more word out of either of you,' she warned, 'and you're going to be riding by yourselves. Is that clear?'

Her brothers nodded sullenly and said no more.

Still they climbed. The trail was steeper now — the air thinner. Breathing became more difficult and their exhaled breath clouded before them. They passed through two nameless mining camps, the steep rocky slopes dotted with crude makeshift shacks and sluices worked by bearded, grim-faced men; suspicious men, none of whom knew of or had seen the Blackthorns or anyone who resembled them.

They rode on, cutting through a narrow pass that descended into a broad valley that was home to several ranches. Here and there log-houses showed among the trees and thick-coated horses, sheep and goats grazed on the grass. Mingled in with the domestic animals were wild elk, their wide-spread, many-pointed antlers making them easy to distinguish. Skirting them, the Indian led Lawless and the Kincannons across the valley. They kept within sight of the river, following its winding path until they came to Peck's Store. Smoke spiraled up from the stone chimney, while horses, pack-mules and a loaded freight wagon pulled by oxen were tied up in front of the popular one-room, log trading post.

Reining up a short distance from it, Lawless and the Indian dismounted and handed their reins to Mercy. 'You three stay here,' Lawless told them.

'What if they're in there?' Jonah said.

'An' what if they start shootin'?' added Caleb. 'Don't you want us to help?'

'No,' Lawless said firmly. 'That's the last thing I want.' Then to Mercy: 'First sign of trouble, you an' your brothers take cover in those trees there,' he pointed, 'or behind those rocks. An' don't come out till I signal you to, okay?'

Mercy nodded and nervously brushed her bangs aside. 'If they're not in there,' she said, 'don't stay too long. Looks like a big storm's headed our way.'

Lawless looked up at the black clouds gathering overhead. The sun had already dipped below the range of flat-topped mountains, and in the distance the faint growl of thunder could be heard.

'Tonight we must sleep on high ground,' Shadow Wolf said, 'else we wake drowning.'

'Amen,' Lawless said.

Hitching up his gun-belt, he accompanied the old Indian to the trading post. As they walked Shadow Wolf studied the countless hoof-prints and wagon tracks on the ground. Beside him, Lawless kept his hand on his six-gun and his eyes trained on the door. But no one came out and after a thorough search of the muddy ground surrounding the small log building Shadow Wolf turned to Lawless and shook his head.

Lawless sighed, relieved and disappointed at the same time. Thunder again rumbled faintly beyond the mountains. 'This won't take long,' he told the Indian. 'Get the young'uns mounted up an' ready to ride.'

The old Lakota nodded and started back toward Mercy and her brothers.

'Hey,' Lawless said. Then as the Indian looked at him: 'You got a bottle hid?'

'No. Why you ask, citizen?'

'Just wonderin'. You know. Why you ain't got the shakes?'

'I make pact with Takuskanskan — '

'Taku — who?'

'Takuskanskan, Lakota guardian spirit from stars.'

'What kind of pact?'

'He make me forget about whiskey if after we find girl with fire in her hair I go with him to spirit world.'

Lawless frowned. ''Mean you die?'

'No. Not die. Live forever.' The old Lakota turned and plodded on toward Mercy and her brothers.

Lawless shook his head, bemused, and entered the trading post.

Inside, men of all ages and professions sat warming themselves around a pot-belly stove. As they passed around a jug of whiskey, each one tried to out-lie the others with tall tales. Most of them had pipes and the air was thick with smoke. A dozen different, familiar odors flooded Lawless' senses, dominated by the smell of bacon frying, coffee, and pine logs burning.

He glanced around but did not recognize anyone in the crowd. Satisfied

189

he was not going to get shot in the back, he elbowed his way to the counter behind which stood a large, bulky, balding man with a scraggly beard that hung down like a yellow bib over his green plaid shirt. His left cheek bulged with snuff and as he stood there, his massive hairy arms folded across his chest, every so often he leaned forward and spit into an upturned coffee can. He then went on listening to two tall, gaunt trappers in furs who were sharing a jug at the counter. They stopped talking and all three warily eyed Lawless as he elbowed his way through the crowd and joined them.

'Help you, friend?'

'Hope so,' Lawless said affably. 'I'm lookin' for my uncle . . . figured maybe he'd passed this way.'

'An' who might be your uncle, mister?'

'Name's Jules Blackthorn. He's with his four boys, my cousins.' Lawless described Blackthorn and his sons, adding: 'We were s'posed to leave

Cheyenne together. But I tied one on an' ended up a guest of the law. Uncle Jules said he'd wait till I got out, but for some reason he an' his sons took off the next mornin'. I've ridden my horse almost into the ground tryin' to catch up with 'em, but what with the damn rain an' a thrown shoe, well, I ain't been able to.'

The man behind the counter tried to look sympathetic. 'Sorry, mister, they ain't been in here. How 'bout you boys?' he asked the two trappers. 'You run into anyone like that on your way in?'

Both men hesitated, just long enough to make Lawless suspicious, and shook their heads. 'How 'bout a snort?' one of them said, offering Lawless the jug. 'When this storm hits, reckon you'll need it.'

Lawless balanced the jug on his shoulder and took a swig that burned all the way down. 'Thank you kindly,' he said. Nodding goodbye, he turned and squeezed through the jostling crowd to the door. As he opened it, he glanced back at the three men, and caught them talking about him. They quickly turned away, but by their guilty looks he sensed they had lied to him and wondered why.

Outside, the rapidly approaching storm had brought darkness early and Lawless felt light rain spitting on his face. He looked around for Mercy and her brothers and realized they were now grouped around Shadow Wolf, who was on his knees peering at the ground alongside the trading post. Lawless hurried over to them. 'Find somethin'?' he asked the Indian.

'They came this way!' blurted Caleb.

'An' they crossed the river,' added Jonah. 'Didn't they, Shadow Wolf?'

The old Lakota looked up and nodded. 'It is possible,' he admitted.

Lawless hunkered down and looked at the two hoof-prints indicated by the Indian. 'This it?' he asked. 'Just these two?'

Shadow Wolf shook his head and

pointed in the direction of the river. 'I count twelve altogether.'

'Twelve? Why only twelve?'

'Not know for sure.'

'You're the tracker. Take a guess.'

'Four other horses following trample over them.'

Lawless nodded, accepting the logical reason. 'Five scalpers, five different prints — could be them all right.'

'What about Cinny?' Mercy asked. 'Where's her horse?'

'Reckon they got rid of it.'

'' Mean she's riding double?'

'That'd be my guess,' Lawless said. Rising, he kept bent over and followed the tracks that led toward the river. Coming to the last two prints, he stopped and examined them carefully. Both prints were cast in sun-dried mud. Though not perfect, they did show caulk marks and two tiny protrusions to the left of the front mark that resembled the letters K and S.

'You satisfied it's them?' he asked the Indian.

Shadow Wolf shrugged. 'Your eyes see what I see. Two marks. Both to the left of the caulks. Reasonable assumption. That is all I know, citizen.'

'Are we going after them?' Mercy asked eagerly.

Thunder rumbled overhead, closer now.

'Not tonight,' Lawless said, as the rain increased. 'Right now, only thing we're gonna do is find some high ground. An' fast!'

24

The valley was largely flat and cover was meager. What trees there were stood on level ground, offering protection from the rain but not from any potential flooding should the river overflow.

With few choices, they finally settled on a large rocky overhang that protruded from the side of a steep hill. Already rainwater was running down on both sides of the overhang, but so far at least the level area that formed a ledge under it remained dry. Dismounting at the base of the hill, the rain now hammering on their slickers, they scrambled upward, dragging their reluctant horses behind them.

It was not easy. The storm was close now and the steady downpour made the ground slippery. Worse, the repeated cracks of thunder scared the horses, making them hard to handle. Even the normally-docile pack-mule panicked, braying and kicking at anyone who came close. Cursing it, Lawless turned his horse over to Shadow Wolf, grabbed the mule's lead-rope, 'C'mon, you stubborn, lug-headed sonofabitch,' and tried to lead it up the hill. It balked, digging its forelegs into the ground so that Lawless could not move it.

Above him, halfway up the hill, the others had reached the ledge under the overhang. Shadow Wolf, seeing Lawless' predicament, left Mercy and her brothers to hobble the horses and started back down the hillside.

Lawless watched him, marveling at the old Lakota's nimbleness, but at the same time wondering what use he would be. He hadn't long to wait. On reaching him, Shadow Wolf removed the rain-soaked blanket from about his shoulders and threw it over the mule's head. Unable to see, the animal stopped kicking and stood there, trembling. The old Indian unfastened his rawhide belt and quickly tied it around the blanket so that it wouldn't fall off.

'Give me gun,' he told Lawless. 'You take rope.'

'I ain't draggin' no dead mule up that hill,' Lawless said, misunderstanding.

Lightning flashed. Thunder cracked overhead, making the mule jump.

'No time to argue, citizen,' Shadow Wolf said. 'Take rope!'

Grudgingly, Lawless handed him the six-gun and grabbed the lead-rope. Shadow Wolf moved behind the mule, held the Colt against the mule's rump, barrel pointed away from him — and fired.

The bullet creased the mule's rump, burning the animal. Startled, it brayed and leapt forward, almost bumping into Lawless, and blindly scrambled upward.

Keeping ahead of the mule, Lawless kept climbing up the slope, shouting encouragement when it slowed and tugging on the rope so its momentum didn't stall.

It turned out to be a violent, virulent storm. Though it had approached rapidly, once it reached the valley it slowed down, hovering overhead as if it had a personal vendetta to settle, punishing everything below with a frighteningly dazzling display of lightning, deafening thunder and torrential rain.

The overhang, a massive slab of granite that protruded some eight feet from the hillside, and a similar distance above the ledge, at first offered Lawless and the others protection from the downpour. But as the wind increased, it blew the rain sideways, slashing across the huddled group like wet knives.

The storm seemed to take forever to move on. At last though, sometime after midnight, the blackest of the clouds broke up and drifted eastward, taking the thunder and lightning with them. The wind lessened, no longer whipping the treetops, and as the sky lightened the rain began to slacken off until it became nothing more than a steady drizzle.

Rising, Lawless shook the rain off his slicker then cautiously moved to the edge of the ledge and peered out at the inky darkness. Despite the lack of a moon the floor of the valley on both sides of the river shimmered as if it were alive. Lawless frowned and took a longer look, realizing suddenly that the ground was flooded and that what he saw shimmering was actually water.

'We got trouble,' he said, beckoning to the others. Then, as they joined him: 'Looks like most of the valley's underwater.'

'Will it go away by morning, do you think?' Mercy asked.

'Doubt it. The ground was already saturated. 'Less we feel like swimmin', we could be here a day or two.'

'B-But what about Cinny?' Jonah said. 'Shadow Wolf said those tracks he found looked pretty fresh.'

'Yeah,' Caleb chimed in, 'we don't keep after them, they could get so far ahead we'll never catch 'em.'

'We caught them once,' Lawless

reminded him. 'We'll do it again. Anyways, it ain't like we got a choice.'

'Maybe it's not deep,' Mercy said. 'Maybe it's just a few inches and then we can wade through it.'

'Not wade across river,' the old Indian said. 'Water too deep, move too fast.'

'I don't care!' Jonah said. 'You can do what you please. But Cinny's my sister an' I'm going after her.'

'Me too,' Caleb said. 'We don't get her away from those scalpers, no telling what they'll do to her.'

Lawless wanted to say that anything the scalpers had intended to do to Cinnamon, they would have done by now. But he saw no reason to upset Mercy or her brothers any further. So instead he said: 'No point in thinkin' about that, son. It'll just get your mind all twisted. Anyways,' he continued, 'maybe you're right. Maybe come daylight the water *will* go away. Meanwhile, there's still a few hours 'fore dawn. Let's try to get some rest.'

* * *

But when daylight came the valley was still flooded. The water was only ankle-deep in most places, but for about fifty yards on both sides of the fast-moving, debris-strewn river Lawless judged it was at least up to a man's waist. When the brothers challenged him on that, he pointed at a stand of young cedars along the near bank. The trees were six to eight feet high and the water was almost halfway up their trunks.

'How deep you reckon it is?' he said when they looked glum.

'Too deep,' Mercy said before they could answer. 'Ben's right. We'll have to stay here at least until tomorrow.'

Shadow Wolf, who had been looking off downriver, said: 'Ferry not cross today. Water too fast.'

'Ferry?' Lawless squinted in the direction the Indian was looking. 'Where do you see — ?'

'There,' pointed Mercy. ''Longside

201

those big trees. See it?'

Everyone saw it now, a small log shack beside the river. The water had risen several feet up all four walls and its owner, wearing a dripping hat and a yellow slicker, sat hunched over on the sloping roof. With one arm clutching a bedraggled brown mutt, he was looking down at the ferry raft floating in the water below him. One end of the raft was wedged against a tree and the other attached to a heavy pull-rope that stretched across the swollen river to the opposite landing.

'I bet that's how the scalpers crossed,' Caleb said.

'An' we'll cross the same way,' Lawless said, 'soon as the ferryman figures it's safe.'

'Bet he'd take us 'cross right now if we paid him enough,' Jonah said.

'Money no good if drowned,' Shadow Wolf said.

'What little money we have,' Mercy said to Jonah, 'is to feed us, not waste on bribing a ferryman to risk his life, and ours, crossing a river that we could all drown in. And that's the truth of it.'

'No use talkin' to them,' Jonah said to his brother. 'They don't care if Cinny lives or dies.' He started to turn away but Mercy angrily grabbed him, spun him around so he was facing her.

'You ever say that again,' she warned, 'and you won't have me for a sister!'

Pushing him aside, she stormed over to the horses. Though her face was hidden, they could hear her crying.

Lawless thrust his face into Jonah's. 'You got a sorry mouth, boy!' Then as the youth glared sullenly at him: 'Now take your foot out of it an' go apologize.'

'You ain't my Pa,' Jonah said. 'I don't have to do what you tell me.'

'Thanks for remindin' me,' Lawless said. He bent down and before anyone realized what he was doing, he grabbed Jonah's ankles and jerked them backward. Jonah gave a startled cry and fell forward, over the ledge. He would have plunged headlong down the steep, muddy hillside but Lawless kept hold of his ankles and thrusting his arms straight out, held Jonah up in the air.

Gasping with fear, Jonah stopping struggling and begged Lawless not to drop him.

'Can't hear you,' Lawless said. 'All that infernal thunder last night made me deaf.'

'Put him down,' Caleb hissed. He had grabbed the Winchester leaned against the rocks and now aimed it at Lawless. 'Put him down or I'll shoot you.'

'Go ahead,' Lawless said calmly.

'Shoot him,' Shadow Wolf said, 'and your brother dies on rocks below.'

Caleb hesitated, not sure what to do next.

Mercy approached, sniffing back her tears. 'Don't do it, Ben,' she begged. 'Please. You've scared him enough. Put him down.'

'Only if he apologizes.'

'I do, I do,' yelled Jonah. 'I . . . I . . . I'm sorry, sis. Honest!'

Lawless stepped back from the edge

and dropped Jonah to the ground. 'From now on,' he warned, 'keep your mouth shut and try to think smart.'

There was nothing to make a fire with on the ledge, so they breakfasted on cold beans and venison jerky. The morning turned bright and sunny. The floodwater covering the valley floor gradually retreated, leaving the ground soggy and muddy, but the banks of the river remained flooded by waist-deep water.

Out on the river bushes and uprooted trees were swept along by the fast-moving current. The ferryman and his mutt were no longer on the roof. Sometime during the night or early dawn they had managed to climb down and now the mutt was sitting on the raft watching as his master checked the condition of the pull-ropes.

'How long you think 'fore we can cross?' Caleb asked Lawless.

'Tomorrow maybe. All depends on the river an' when the ferryman figures — '

'I know, I know; that it's safe.'

'What if we were to ride downriver some?' Jonah said. He, like the others, was sitting on the ledge watching the ferryman work. 'Maybe there's other places where it ain't so deep?'

Lawless turned to the Indian. 'You've been here before. Tell him.'

'This safest place to cross when river deep.'

Frustrated, Jonah got up and joined his brother, who was sitting near the horses.

'Don't be angry with him,' Mercy said to Lawless. 'He and Caleb, they love Cinny very much and — '

' — feel so goddamn helpless, yeah I know the feelin',' Lawless said. 'To be this close an' yet so far, can twist a fella's brains so's he can't think straight. What worries me most,' he added, looking at the brothers, 'is that one of 'em will do somethin' impulsive an' end up slowin' us down even more.'

'I could talk to them,' Mercy said. 'But I doubt if it would do much good.'

Lawless didn't answer. Deep in thought for a moment, he then said to Shadow Wolf: 'Feel like gettin' wet?'

'I not try to swim 'cross river, if that is what you mean.'

Lawless chuckled. 'Hadn't thought of that, but now you mention it . . . ' He chuckled again, turned and picked up his saddle.

The old Lakota rolled his eyes at Mercy, 'White Eyes! . . . I will be with Guardian Spirit before I understand you,' and followed after Lawless.

25

Watched from the ledge by Mercy, Jonah and Caleb, Lawless and Shadow Wolf cautiously led their saddled horses down the muddy hillside. It was a dangerous descent. Several times the men and their horses slipped and almost lost their footing, and by the time they safely reached the base of the hill they were spattered with mud. Mounting, they rode in the direction of the ferry.

'It ain't right,' Jonah grumbled, 'not lettin' us go with 'em.'

'You heard Ben's reason,' Mercy said. 'He wanted you to stay here and protect me, in case something happened to him or Shadow Wolf.'

'That's just grownup talk,' Caleb said contemptuously, 'to make us feel important.'

'You *are* important,' Mercy said.

'You're the two most important people in my life. If something happened to you, either of you, I don't know what I'd do.'

'Nothing's gonna happen to us,' Jonah assured her, 'so quit worryin', sis.' He hugged her then stepped back and looked down at Lawless, adding: 'Sure glad you didn't marry him, though.'

Mercy didn't answer. But as she watched Lawless and the old Indian riding slowly toward the river, she thought: *I could do a lot worse.*

* * *

The ferryman looked surprised to see two riders approaching. He was even more surprised to see that one of them was an old, shriveled, crinkly-faced Indian in muddy, store-bought clothes whose braided gray hair was streaked with white. The other, the young, leaner, wide-shouldered man, sat tall and easy in the saddle. Yet there was a cat-like tautness about him that the ferryman, who in his profession had seen just about every kind of man, knew was the trademark of men who lived by their guns — guns that, like this man, were easy to draw from tied-down holsters.

Wondering what this unlikely couple was doing together, especially in this part of the country, he watched them ride closer.

They were now riding through muddy water that reached up to their horses' bellies and all around them swirled uprooted bushes and broken branches. As they got closer, the ferryman stopped hammering on a piece of wood that lent support to a sign reading HIMLEY'S FERRY and waved and hollered to them.

'Don't come no closer. River's tore up big holes in the ground. Your horse steps in one an' next thing you know, current's got you an' you're fightin' to keep your head above water.'

'Thanks for the warnin', mister.'

Lawless and Shadow Wolf reined up. They were now only twenty feet from the ferryman, and could see, just below the surface, a rope looped around his waist that snaked out behind him and was fastened to one of the landing posts. The ferry raft, no longer wedged against the cabin, was now was tied up alongside the landing. It bobbed dangerously up and down on the surging waves, held in position by the thick pull-rope that spanned the angry white-capped river, its ends knotted around the opposite landing posts.

'Hope you two ain't figurin' on me takin' you 'crost,' the ferryman said, indicating the water swirling around his powerful chest. 'As you can see, river's just waitin' to drown somebody.'

'Won't be us,' Lawless said. 'We just want to know if you got some idea of how long it'll be 'fore we *can* cross.'

'Hard to tell,' the ferryman said. 'Seen it where it took two weeks for the river to get back to normal, other times just one or two days. One thing's for sure though — won't be till the day after tomorrow earliest.' He gazed out at the fast-flowing river. 'Reminds me of this woman I once wintered with; unpredictable as hell an' happy to cause you grief when you least expect it.'

Shadow Wolf's stoic expression never changed. 'Anywhere up or downriver safe to cross now?' he asked.

'Not 'less you're a trout or a beaver. An' I wouldn't even count on it then.'

'Reckon we'll just have to wait it out then. Thanks, mister,' Lawless tipped his hat, then he and the Indian turned their horses around and rode back to the hill.

Later, sitting on the ledge with their backs against the rocks Jonah and Caleb scowled as Lawless related what the ferryman had told them.

'Don't look like that,' Mercy told them. 'Like Ben already said, we caught up with those devils before and we'll do it again.'

Lawless expected one or both of the brothers to react disagreeably. Instead, they shrugged as if it meant nothing to them.

'Whatever you say, sis,' Jonah said. 'Reckon we'll just have to wait an' hope for the best.'

'Yeah,' Caleb agreed. 'An' while we're waitin', maybe tomorrow or the next day we can shoot one of them big fat elk down there,' he thumbed at a small herd of elk grazing near the base of the hill. 'That way, when we do get to ridin' again, we'll have meat to go with our beans.'

'That's a fine idea,' Lawless said. 'Let's plan on cuttin' one out in the mornin', right after first light when they're feedin'. Oh, an' one other thing,' he added. 'Horses need to eat more than those handfuls of oats we fed 'em. Figure we should take them down to the valley now an' let 'em fill their bellies with that fresh sweet grass — '

'All night, you mean?' Mercy asked. Then as Lawless nodded: 'But what if they wander off or the wolves get them? I heard some howling last night.'

'Me, too,' Jonah said. 'Maybe one of us should sleep down there with them. 'Long as we keep a fire burnin' we oughtn't to have no problem with wolves.'

'Any problem,' Mercy corrected out of habit.

'Any problem,' Jonah said affably.

'Now that's thinkin' smart,' Lawless said, clapping him on the back. 'Tell you what: I'll take the first watch, Shadow Wolf can spell me after a few hours — '

' — an' me'n Caleb can spell him,' Jonah said. 'By then it'll be sunup and we can bring the horses back up here if need be.'

26

That night when the moon came out, so too did the wolves. Lawless listened to their mournful howling as he stoked the fire, sending a shower of sparks shooting up into the darkness. The horses heard the howling too. It caused them to snicker and flick their tails uneasily as they munched on the grass close to Lawless' bedroll. He levered a cartridge into magazine of his Winchester and leaned the rifle against his saddle in case the wolves got bold enough to attack. Then, tugging his jacket collar around his already-numb ears, he pulled the blanket up under his chin and warmed his gloved hands around his coffee mug.

It was approaching midnight and while he waited for Shadow Wolf to relieve him, his mind wandered back to Texas and he wondered what his outlaw cousin, Will, was doing: Enjoying himself with some pretty, fat-assed, melon-breasted Mexican whore in a cantina or hotel room south of the border, no doubt.

Lawless shook his head, half-disgusted, half-tolerant of his cousin's wild and rebellious behavior. He, himself, had once been as rowdy and belligerently quick-tempered as Will; hell, he'd even cut notches in the grip of his six-gun to show everyone that killing a man meant nothing to him.

But it *did* mean something. And eventually it ate away at him enough so that he couldn't deny it any longer. And when his cousin had tried to enroll him in his gang of bank-robbing border trash, Lawless turned him down.

But that gnawed at him too and he was considering changing his mind, when the only woman — he'd sworn when she died he would never say her name again — he'd ever truly loved stepped into his life —

A noise among the trees behind him

disturbed his thoughts. Turning, he peered into the darkness, expecting to see the old Indian appear, but instead it was Caleb, carrying his rifle, who stepped into the firelight.

'What're you doin' here?' Lawless began.

Then something hard struck the back of his head and he pitched forward into inky silence.

★ ★ ★

The next thing he remembered was someone shaking him. He opened his eyes and through a blurry haze saw dark gentle eyes peering out of a walnut at him. He blinked and the walnut turned into Shadow Wolf's face. Lawless squeezed his brows together, blinked again and shook away the cobwebs.

'Brothers gone,' the old Lakota said. 'Their horses, too.'

'Figures . . . ' Lawless gingerly touched the back of his head, wincing

217

as pain shot through him. 'How long ago? You got any idea?'

'Not more than ten minute. Old age, it is a cruel thing.'

'What's gettin' old got to do with anythin'?'

'As a young brave I could hear a butterfly breathing. Now I sleep with the ears of the dead.'

'Ain't your fault, *amigo*. It's mine. I knew somethin' was wrong when those boys didn't get riled up after I told them it was goin' to be two more days 'fore we could cross. Does Mercy know?' Lawless added.

'No. She still sleeping when I come here.'

'Just as well.' Lawless looked toward the river. 'Maybe we can round 'em up 'fore they manage to drown themselves.'

Still groggy he got to his feet, swayed briefly and steadied himself. By then Shadow Wolf had already picked up his saddle, thrown it on the buckskin's back and was tightening the cinch.

'You're some old man,' Lawless said admiringly.

'Remember that, citizen, when you pay me off with whiskey,' the old Lakota said. But he was smiling when he said it and Lawless chuckled, despite himself.

Just then a rifle shot came from the river. Exchanging grim looks, they swung up on their horses and spurred them toward the ferry.

When they reached the ferryman's cabin the banks were still flooded but the water level had lowered since their last visit; it now only reached up to the big man's knees.

On recognizing Lawless and Shadow Wolf, he pointed with his rifle at the raft that was now halfway across the river. It had been overturned by the churning waters and pitched up and down as the current tried to tear it from the pull-rope.

'Goddamn fools!' he yelled. 'Bastards stole my raft . . . tried to make it 'crost the river on their own!'

Lawless squinted in the darkness and could just make out a figure struggling to hang onto the side of the raft. He looked on the other side, hoping to see another figure clinging there, but could see no one. His heart sank. He tried to make out which brother had survived, but with waves splashing over the figure and the current trying to pull him under, Lawless could not tell if it was Jonah or Caleb.

Not wasting another moment, he jumped from his horse and waded to the landing.

'Wait!' the ferryman shouted. 'Come back! You can't save him, mister!'

'Can try,' Lawless yelled. He caught hold of the pull-rope that was still tied to the landing post and hauled himself, hand over hand, out over the river. His weight pulled the rope lower and the icy water rose up around his chest. The cold took his breath away. Worse, the undertow grabbed him like a giant hand, pulling at him, dragging the lower half of his body violently sideways, forcing him to grip the rope even harder. Waves pounded him, water splashing over his face so that he could not see what was ahead.

Not daring to let go of the rope with either hand, he shook his head and kept blinking until he could make out the raft some twenty feet in front of him. It was thrashing around in the surging water, the weight of the tied-together-logs jerking at the rope, threatening to rip it from his grasp. But he clung on grimly and with great effort, gradually hauled himself closer and closer to the raft.

He could now see that it was Jonah who had survived. Lawless shouted to him, yelling out his name, but got no response. He watched as the exhausted youth desperately clung to the edge of the violently-pitching raft. But his strength was failing and Lawless knew he had to get to him quickly, or lose him to the river.

Hauling himself along the rope until he was only a few feet from the raft,

Lawless again shouted his name. This time Jonah heard him. He turned his head and on seeing Lawless, screamed something at him. His words were hidden by the pounding water. But Lawless nodded as if he heard them and saw relief mixed with terror on Jonah's face. It gave him the strength to haul himself along the last few feet of rope.

Now only an arm's length from Jonah, Lawless pulled his legs out of the water and crossed them over the rope. In this sloth-like fashion, he inched himself forward until he was directly over the raft and Jonah; then lowering his legs so that they hung over the boy's head, he yelled: 'Grab hold of me! I'll pull you up!'

Jonah stared fearfully at Lawless, but didn't move.

'Hurry!' Lawless shouted. 'Grab my legs!'

Jonah hesitated, still frozen with fear.

'Do it! *Now*, goddammit! You'll drown if you don't!'

Jonah hesitated another moment then let go of the raft with one hand and grabbed at Lawless' dangling feet. Lawless felt the boy's fingers grasp around one ankle. He looked down — in time to see Jonah let go of the raft with his free hand and try to grasp Lawless' boot with it. For an infinitesimal moment his fingers closed around the toe of the boot, but then the surging water swung his body sideways, leaving Jonah hanging by one hand.

Lawless opened his fingers a little around the rope and strained to lower himself even more. But it was hopeless: he felt Jonah's fingers slipping from his boot and even as he looked down he saw the Kincannon boy sucked under then swept away by the swirling current.

Without hesitation, Lawless let go of the rope and dropped into the river. The raging deep closed over his head, tumbling him over and over, crushing the breath from him and sweeping him downriver.

27

Unable to see anything, Lawless powered himself to the surface. As his head burst above the water, he gulped in fresh air, at the same time thrashing his arms and legs in an effort not to be dragged under again.

Dark trees and bushes lined both sides of the river. Carried along by the swift-moving current, he fought to keep himself above water. Ahead, he could see rocks poking up, with white-water churning over them. Lawless used his arms like paddles, safely steering himself between the jagged rocks. Waves battered his face, making it impossible to see clearly. Even so, he managed to get glimpses of both banks, hoping as he did to see Jonah or Caleb clinging onto a bush or tree.

He never saw Caleb but after a hundred yards or so the water grew less turbulent and Lawless, spotting an opening between the trees, wearily swam to the nearest bank. Dragging himself ashore, he waded inland a short distance until he reached dry ground. There, he collapsed on his back in the mud and lay there, chest heaving, heart pounding, staring at the stars as he tried to regain his breath.

After a little he sat up, clasped his hands about his knees and looked out at the fast-moving river. He had no idea how long he sat there. All he could think about was how much he dreaded the thought of having to tell Mercy that both of her brothers were dead.

A noise in the trees and bushes to his left interrupted his thinking. He listened and realized it was a horse approaching from downriver. He turned toward the sound and after a few moments saw a rider emerging from the trees.

It was Shadow Wolf. Someone was clinging on behind him and as they drew close Lawless recognized the bedraggled rider as . . . Jonah!

Relieved, he jumped up and as the old Indian reined up beside him, grasped the bridle. 'Jesus-on-a-cross,' he exclaimed. 'Am I glad to see you!'

'H-He saved my life,' Jonah said shakily.

'Not true,' the old Lakota said, reverting to pidgin English. 'Horse run away with me. River spit boy out. I bring him here.'

Lawless sighed. 'I'm too tired to call you a liar, old man, but one day we're goin' to sit down an' talk 'bout this.' To Jonah he said: 'You're safe, son, that's all that matters.'

'What about Caleb? Where is he, do you know?'

Lawless shook his head. 'Was he on the raft with you?'

'Yes. But he fell off 'fore I did an' . . . an' . . . I tried to save him . . . honest . . . but . . . but the water was movin' too fast an' it . . . dragged his hand out of mine an' . . .'

He broke down, sobbing.

Lawless looked at Shadow Wolf, who

slowly shook his head.

'We'd better head back,' Lawless said grimly. ''Fore Mercy wakes up an' wonders where the hell everyone is.'

'B-But what about Caleb?' Jonah said through his tears.

'Come daylight, we'll all start lookin' for him.'

With a curt nod to the Indian to follow, Lawless started back toward the ferry.

28

By morning the water level had dropped even lower, allowing the four of them to ride closer to the banks of the still-swollen river as they searched for Caleb or any trace of his body.

No one spoke. It seemed senseless. Everything had been said the night before when Lawless had told Mercy that her brother, Caleb, was missing, and possibly drowned. He had done it alone, insisting that Jonah stay with Shadow Wolf and the horses at the base of the hill while he climbed up to the ledge and gave her the potentially tragic news.

Shocked, she sat there staring blankly at him as if her brain was incapable of accepting such horrendous news. Then she numbly shook her head, kept on shaking it as she said softly, almost inaudibly: 'No, no, no . . . not Caleb

. . . no, no, no, it's a mistake . . . he can't be missing . . . you must be mistaken . . . he's probably just lost . . . all that water . . . nobody could find their way back . . . nobody!'

'You could be right,' Lawless said gently. 'I mean it *is* possible. There's always that chance, however remote, that he could have swum ashore.'

'Yes,' she said. 'Yes, that's exactly what he did.'

'I just don't want you to get your hopes up too much . . . not with the river runnin' high an' fast like it is.'

'I don't care,' she said firmly. 'I don't care if the waters of hell run in that river. I will never believe Caleb is dead. And that's the truth of it.'

Lawless didn't know what else to say. He'd expected her to be emotional, to sob her heart out and adamantly deny that her brother was drowned, like most people would. But here she was, not a tear in her eyes, not a trace of grief in her expression, just the same stubborn determination he had seen her display when her father was about to whip her; her eyes ablaze, her pale lips set tight and thin, her jaw out-thrust, her voice calm and practical as if she believed she could will whatever it was that was threatening her or her family away.

Nor did she feel any different the next morning, when at sunup Lawless led her down the steep muddy hillside to the small stand of trees where Shadow Wolf and Jonah were already saddling the horses. On seeing her, Jonah broke down. Hugging her, he tearfully started to blame himself for everything, especially his brother drowning, but she cut him off.

'Stop it!' she said angrily. 'Caleb did not drown. And I won't have you talking like he did. Your brother is alive. He may be hurt, he may be wandering around lost, but he's out there somewhere. Alive! And I assure you, we *will* find him!'

But though they spent the entire day riding alongside the calmer but still-flooded river, searching among the trees, bushes and rocks for any trace of Caleb, or clues that might reveal where he had gone, they found nothing to give them any hope that he had swum ashore and was still alive.

Dusk fell. By now they were all weary and their spirits dragged. Even Mercy seemed to have lost some of her unflagging resolve. Lawless reined up in a sheltered gully that was littered with old blackened fire pits and broken furniture cast off long ago by settlers and wagons trains headed west and suggested they make camp here.

'Then, come mornin',' he added, 'we can figure out if we want to go on searchin' this side or go back to the ferry, cross the river an' start lookin' on the other.'

He was addressing Mercy and Jonah more than the Indian, who rarely questioned his decisions, and both Kincannons shrugged as if they didn't care.

'All right, then,' Lawless said, dismounting. 'Let's get at it.'

Sending Shadow Wolf to shoot something for supper, and Jonah to collect brush that they could put between their bedrolls and the damp ground, Lawless unsaddled the horses while Mercy tried to start a fire. It wasn't easy. The wood she found was still wet and would not light at first; then, when eventually it did, it smoked so badly her eyes watered.

As if that were the final straw, she suddenly started crying. She cried without sound and Lawless might never have noticed her tears if he hadn't taken out the old newspaper in his saddlebag that he used instead of leaves, and offered it to her to help make the fire burn.

'I'm n-not crying,' she said quickly as he hunkered down across from her. 'It's all this smoke . . . it's making my eyes water.'

'Mine too,' Lawless said diplomatically. They sat there in awkward silence for a while, neither knowing what to say. Then as Mercy dried her eyes on her sleeve, he said: 'Okay if I make a suggestion . . . ?'

Mercy nodded and loudly sniffed back her tears.

'Tomorrow, if the water's gone down enough an' the ferry's back to workin', we should cross the river an' start lookin' for your sister again.'

Without meeting his eyes, she said dully: 'You think Caleb's dead, don't you?'

'Didn't say that. Truth is, Mercy, I don't know what to think.'

'But you want to give up looking for him?'

'Not give up exactly . . . more like put it on hold for a spell.'

'Leave him in the Good Lord's hands, that it?'

Lawless chewed on his thoughts for a moment before answering. 'My Pa used to tell a story at prayer meetings sometimes. He wasn't a preacher or nothin', but he was a good man, mostly honest, an' folks respected his opinion. He told about this feller who asked

233

God to help him solve this particular problem he had. God, who was busy solving the rest of the world's problems, agreed. 'Give it to me, my son, and I'll see what I can do.' Well, the feller waited an' waited an' finally, bein' human, lost his patience, took his problem back an' demanded to know why God hadn't helped him. God shrugged an' said: ''Cause you didn't give me time to.''

Mercy took several moments to absorb his words. Then she pinned him with her eyes and said: 'What about my sister? You think we should leave her fate to God, too?'

Lawless realized he didn't and his hypocrisy embarrassed him. 'Reckon you got me there,' he admitted.

Mercy nodded, as if expecting his answer, and said wistfully: 'You and Momma would have seen eye-to-eye.'

'How so?'

'Well, she didn't have a story like your father, but she did believe that even God needs a little push now and then.'

'Amen,' Lawless said. He looked across the flames at Mercy and found her smiling at him. It was a pure, trusting smile, innocent as a nun, and it transcended all of their troubles, warming him even more than the fire.

29

The next morning the ferry carried them across the river. The ground here was mostly dried out, though many of the tree trunks were still caked with mud, but the flood had washed away all the hoof-prints and wagon-wheel-ruts and the Indian did not even bother to look for the scalpers' tracks until they were several miles from the river.

At first he didn't find any. Then, as the trail climbed higher into the Rockies, hoof-prints appeared in the dirt. They were all shod, making it almost impossible to know if they belonged to horses or mules, but due to the wheel ruts that had rolled over them Shadow Wolf guessed it was a team of mules pulling a freight or ore wagon up the mountain.

They rode on, ever-upward. After a little the old Lakota stopped to relieve himself. His companions continued on. He caught up to them a few minutes later and took over the lead again, head crooked sideways as he studied the ground.

They were now above nine thousand feet and the increasing lack of oxygen made them feel sluggish. Every breath was an effort. The kerchiefs they had tied around their faces to combat the cold now became frosty as their quickened breathing dampened them. Dwarfed by the towering mountains they felt strangely small and inadequate, as if they and their stay on earth was no more than a blink of an eye compared to the age of these silent giants.

As they rode on, patches of snow whitened the mountainsides and wind-blown snow flurries swirled around the snowy peaks. At this elevation the cold numbed their red ears and noses and with each labored inhalation chilled their lungs.

Jonah, as usual, was the only one who

complained. First it was about not being able to feel his hands or feet; next how hungry he was; and lastly, how much farther were they going to go without finding any hoof-prints made by the scalpers.

'For all we know we could be headed in the wrong direction,' he said when the others ignored his grumbling. Then, when again no one responded: 'Bet there are hundreds of minin' camps in these mountains. Maybe thousands! We could be months tryin' to find Cinny. Years, even.'

'What would you suggest we do?' Mercy asked him. 'Give up? Look someplace else. Go home? What?'

Jonah shrugged. 'I dunno. Ask him,' he said thumbing at Shadow Wolf. 'He's the tracker.'

'Then let the man track,' Lawless said. 'An' quit runnin' your mouth.'

Ahead, in the distance, they could see a small mining town. The spire of a tiny white church poked above a collection of log- and plank-fronted buildings bordering the trail, while a scattering of crude wooden miners' shacks occupied the hillsides overlooking the town.

Anxious to give their laboring horses a rest they stopped at a little clapboard restaurant with elk antlers mounted over the door. The place needed painting and the door hung on one creaking hinge. But inside was warm and cosy and they sat beside a pot-belly stove and drank hot coffee sweetened with tin milk and wolfed down biscuits-and-gravy.

The bulky, leathery-faced brunette who served them was delighted to have strangers to talk to, and after inquiring about where they were from, 'Wyoming,' and where they were going, 'West,' she finally stopped talking long enough for Lawless to ask her if many other strangers had passed through.

'Not enough to keep me in business,' she said sadly. She spoke with a hand-rolled cigarette slanted from the corner of her red lips, years of constant smoking having stained that side of her face and hair yellow with nicotine. 'Now that most of the mines are played out, an' no one's diggin' for new ones I reckon I'll have to close my doors soon an' move down to Yampa Valley.'

'Reason I ask,' Lawless said, 'is I'm lookin' for my Uncle Jules. A feller in Peck's Store said he an' his four sons mentioned they may be headed up this way.'

'I know most everyone here in Silver Creek,' the woman said. 'What's your uncle's last name?'

'Blackthorn. Jules Blackthorn.'

The woman frowned as she tried to place the name. 'Uh-uh,' she said at last. She put a fresh hand-rolled between her lips, lit it from the butt and inhaled deeply. 'That don't jog my memory none.'

'When did last rain come?' Shadow Wolf asked suddenly.

He had not spoken since entering the restaurant and the woman looked at him as if seeing him for the first time. 'Two — no, three days ago. Had some snow flurries now an' then, but nothing to write home about.'

'Many people pass by since then?'

'Strangers, you mean?'

'Strangers, miners, anyone.'

'No strangers. A few miners — regulars who take their meals here. Why?'

'How far next mine from here?'

'Four miles, give or take. But Silverton's mines are played out too, so I wouldn't figure on findin' your uncle there either,' she added to Lawless.

'I won't,' he said, puzzled by the Indian's questions. 'But thanks, anyway.'

After they finished eating and were gathered in the cold outside the restaurant, Lawless confronted Shadow Wolf. 'Want to tell me what that was all about?'

'I have seen prints that could be the men we hunt,' replied the old Lakota. 'Many prints.'

'When?' Mercy asked. 'Where?'

'Back there,' Shadow Wolf pointed. 'When I stopped to wet the ground.'

'Dammit, why didn't you tell us

before?' Lawless demanded.

'Much depend on what I say,' Shadow Wolf said, giving Jonah a sidelong glance. 'Want to be sure first.'

'When's the last time you saw prints?' Lawless said.

The Indian walked into the street and pointed at hoof-prints in the near-frozen dirt. Lawless, Mercy and Jonah quickly joined him and hunkered down to examine the prints. Made sometime during the day when the dirt was soft and mushy, an early frost now protected them from being trampled flat.

'Couldn't be much plainer than that,' Lawless said indicating the caulk marks and the initial protrusions on each shoe. He looked at the old Lakota, adding: 'Any idea how long ago these were made?'

'If woman tell truth about seeing no strangers, three days ago.'

'After the rain, right?'

Shadow Wolf nodded.

'An' all the prints are headed in the

same direction?' When the Indian nodded again, Lawless straightened up, 'Wait here,' and re-entered the restaurant. They heard him talking to the brunette, but couldn't make out what either of them was saying. Shortly, he rejoined them and said grimly: 'This is the only trail in or out of here.' He glanced up at the hillside, adding: 'Means they're either holed up in one of those shacks or some place in Silverton.'

'How we going to find out which?' Jonah asked.

'Patience,' Shadow Wolf said. Going to his horse, he untied it, mounted, and rode on along the street.

'Where's he going?' Jonah said.

'Give your voice a rest an' get on your horse,' Lawless said sharply. Then to Mercy: 'I ain't goin' to ask you to stay here, 'cause I know you wouldn't anyway. But when we get to Silverton an' corner these weasels they ain't goin' to give up without a fight.'

'I know that,' she said. 'And I know

there's going to be shooting — '

'An' killin',' Lawless reminded. 'You up to that? 'Cause if you ain't, tell me now.'

'Mr. Lawless,' Mercy said, brushing her bangs aside, 'I was ready to kill these 'weasels,' as you call them, when they watered their horses at our cabin. Now that they've got my sister, I'm doubly ready. And that's the truth of it.'

Lawless nodded, satisfied. He looked in the direction of the Indian. Shadow Wolf was now crouched down at the far end of town, examining the ground. After a little he stood up and signaled to Lawless to come ahead. Lawless waved back and then turned to Mercy and Jonah, who were now on their horses.

'There'll be no gunplay till I say so. Got it?'

They nodded. Lawless swung up into the saddle and led them toward the old Indian.

30

Ten years ago Silverton, then known as Silver Town, had been a bawdy, thriving mining camp famous for its rich silver veins. Now it was almost a ghost town. Nearly all of the rundown shacks and mines on the mountain slopes had been abandoned, as had the stores and saloons lining the main street, and the two places still operating — Cole's Eatery and Mobley's Mercantile — had so few customers they were already closed.

Snow flurries greeted Lawless and the others as they rode slowly into town. The tiny white swirling flakes contrasted sharply with the dark of nightfall. But this was no 'Christmas-card' snow; it melted on contact and turned into slush, adding to the already grim, miserable conditions that the few miners still trying to eke out a living endured.

Lawless reined up outside an empty dilapidated wooden building marked ASSAY OFFICE and motioned for everyone to dismount. He then counted the number of shacks on the mountainside in which lights showed. 'I make it five,' he said to the Indian, who was also counting.

Shadow Wolf nodded in accord.

'I didn't see any horses. You?'

'None.'

'If the Blackthorns got here three days ago, like you say, they must have left 'em somewhere.'

'Or turned them loose,' Mercy said.

'Possible. But I doubt it. Not up here. Gets too cold at night. Horses freeze to death too, you know. An' if the Blackthorns are plannin' on ridin' to Texas or somewhere else that's warm, like Jake heard 'em say, they'll need to keep those horses in good shape.'

Mercy pointed up the moonlit street to a building next to a small shuttered church. 'I can't read the sign,' she said, 'but that could be a livery stable.'

'Good eyes,' Lawless said. 'Let's go take a look-see.'

C.J. Crow, according to the faded signs painted on the two-door wooden structure, had once been a Harness Shop, Livery Stable and Blacksmith. Now it was an abandoned eyesore that was slowly being chewed away by mountain winters. There was an alley between the livery and the adjacent church: Lawless led the others into it, dismounted and signaled that he'd be right back. He then ducked around in back.

The rear door, like the front, was kept shut by a Yale & Towne 'cartridge' padlock and rather than wrestle with it, Lawless found a loose board that he forced aside. Peering through the gap he smelled fresh horse dung and, squinting, managed to make out the shapes of five horses. Two were tied up in stalls; the other three roped to a bar along the far wall. He recognized one of the horses, a gray roan with a white-tipped mane and tail, that had been ridden by Jules Blackthorn. The other horses were too nondescript to remember . . . but there were four of them, the same number as Jules' sons.

There was no sign of Cinnamon's horse and Lawless wondered bleakly if she was still with the Blackthorns or had already been sold to someone. The last thought was so depressing, especially after what had happened to Caleb, he decided to keep it to himself.

'Their horses are in there,' he said when he rejoined the others. 'So they're definitely holed up here somewhere.'

'We goin' to bust in on 'em now or wait till morning?' Jonah said.

Lawless looked at him. There was no moon, no street lamps, only the light from the stars. But in the dark of the alley Lawless saw, for the first time since meeting Jonah, some of Mercy's courage and determination on the youth's face.

'What would you do?' he asked.

'Me?'

'Yeah.'

'I ain't in charge.'

'But if you were.'

Jonah chewed his lower lip and looked at his sister.

'Go ahead,' she told him. 'For once have an answer instead of a question.'

Jonah gritted his teeth. 'Tonight,' he said. 'I'd bust in on 'em tonight.'

'I agree,' Lawless said. ''Cept instead of bustin' in on 'em, we're goin' to make them come to us.'

31

After Lawless shot the lock off, he and the Indian hurried into the stable and untied all the horses while Mercy and Jonah kept watch outside. But the shot did not arouse anyone's attention and they were able to herd the horses outside without any problem.

There, they turned them loose and fired two more shots, stampeding the horses down the hill behind the stable. They were soon lost in the darkness.

Lawless signaled to Mercy, Jonah and the Indian to take cover. There was an empty lot on the other side of the church: as one, they ran to it and ducked behind two old, dilapidated, rusty ore wagons that had been left there to rot.

Lawless, meanwhile, entered the stable, flared a match and set fire to a pile of straw in one of the stalls. After doing the same to the straw in the other stalls, he hurried out. Within minutes the stable was ablaze.

Flames shot into the air, lighting up the night. Sparks flew. Some of them landed on the roof of the church and the empty hardware store on the other side. They were afire almost at once.

'I sure hope God doesn't get angry at us for burning His house down,' Mercy said to her brother.

'He's already angry at us,' Jonah said. 'Else He wouldn't have let what's happened happen to us.'

Before she could reply there were shouts in the darkness and men came stumbling out of the lighted cabins. Some of them carried torches, the flames illuminating their faces as they charged down the mountainside.

'It's them!' Mercy hissed at Lawless, who was hiding behind an empty rain barrel.

'I see 'em,' he said, adding: 'Remember what I said: no shootin' till I say.'

Resting his Winchester on top of the

barrel, he lined up the sights on the chest of Jules Blackthorn, tempted even as he did to pull the trigger. But remembering he had left Texas to leave his gunfighter reputation behind, he instead shifted his gaze to the men with Blackthorn, immediately recognizing four of them as the old patriarch's sons. The fifth man was about Blackthorn's age but bigger and black-bearded, and Lawless saw enough of a resemblance to guess it was kin. All wore red long-sleeve undershirts tucked into long johns and boots and carried empty buckets.

Running down the rocky slope alongside them were five other men, similarly dressed and also carrying buckets, who had emerged from the other lighted cabins.

'The horses!' Blackthorn yelled. 'Get the goddamn horses out first!'

Lawless waited till all eleven men had crossed the street and were running to a public water trough then fired a shot that kicked up dirt in front of Blackthorn.

The grizzled old patriarch jerked to a stop, as did the men around him, and everyone turned to see who had fired.

Lawless stepped from behind the rain barrel, rifle aimed at Blackthorn, ready to pull the trigger at the old man's slightest move. 'Don't sweat 'bout the horses,' he called grimly. 'We chased them off 'fore we started the fire.'

'We'd still like to save the rest of the buildings, mister,' one of the men said.

'For what?' Lawless said. 'Posterity?'

He took another step forward, now clearly visible in the glare of the flames. 'All of you — get your hands up!'

The men obeyed. 'We ain't armed,' one of them grumbled. 'Can see that for y'self.'

Lawless saw he was telling the truth. But he kept silent.

''Be damned to hell,' Blackthorn said as he recognized Lawless. 'Never figured on seein' you again, friend.'

'Wasn't high on my list either,'

Lawless said. 'But then, I never figured even pig-suckin' scum like you would stoop to kidnappin'.'

'Kidnappin'?' Jules Blackthorn snorted with amusement. 'You hear that, boys?' he said to his sons. 'Mr. Pureheart, here, thinks we forced the girl to come with us. Tell him how it really went, Joey.'

'Ain't true, mister,' the youngest son, Joey, said. 'When Red thought you was dead, she begged to come with us.'

'Liar!' yelled Jonah. He stood up, his rifle aimed at Joey. 'My sister would *never* go anywhere with someone like you. Any of you!'

As he spoke, Mercy and Shadow Wolf also stood up, guns covering the men at the trough.

'Jonah's right,' Mercy said angrily. 'Cinny's got a wild streak I know, but she'd never run off with the likes of you. *Or* call herself Red. So unless you want me to shoot you right now,' she told Blackthorn, 'tell me where she is!'

'I'll do more'n that, missy. I'll have

Joey go bring her down here so you can ask herself y'self. That okay with you, mister?' he added to Lawless.

Lawless didn't answer. He walked to the nearest of Blackthorn's sons and jammed the Winchester against his ribs. 'Joey ain't back here with Cinnamon by the time I count to a hundred, this boy dies in his place.'

'I can do it, Pa,' Joey said quickly. 'She'll come down here for me.'

Blackthorn nodded. 'Go ahead, boy.' He waited for Joey to sprint off across the street and start scrambling up the mountainside before turning back to Lawless.

'Don't s'pose you'd like to tell me what you done with our horses?'

Lawless said: 'It'll keep till Joey gets back with Cinnamon.'

'Sounds fair,' Blackthorn said. 'Now, how 'bout lettin' us lower our hands. We keep 'em up much longer in this cold, they're likely to never come down.'

Lawless thumbed back the hammer

of the Winchester, at the same time keeping the rifle pressed against Blackthorn's son's ribs. 'Go ahead,' he said. 'Just remember, if you or anyone else even twitches, you'll be buryin' a son.'

32

Lawless had counted to eighty-six when Joey reappeared from one of the shacks. A young slim woman was with him. She wore a white wolf-pelt parka, the hood covering her hair and enough of her face so that no one below could identify her, and white fur gloves. She moved slowly, unsteadily, and had to be coaxed by Joey to continue on down the slope.

'That isn't Cinny,' Jonah exclaimed. 'She doesn't walk like that.'

'She's been feelin' poorly,' Blackthorn explained. 'Must've ate somethin' disagreed with her.'

Lawless watched as Joey helped the woman down the steep muddy slope. 'That's close enough,' he said to Blackthorn as the couple reached the far edge of the street. 'I want to see her hair!'

'Son,' Blackthorn called out. 'Make

her show her hair.'

Joey spoke to the woman. She resisted for a moment and then pushed the hood back off her head, revealing thick flame-red hair that hung past her shoulders.

'Satisfied?' Blackthorn asked. Then as Lawless nodded: 'Come ahead, Joey.'

Joey obeyed.

Blackthorn turned back to Lawless. 'Be much 'bliged if you'd take that rifle out of my boy's ribs.'

'When I'm ready,' Lawless replied. To Mercy he said: 'Ask Cinny if she's all right.'

Mercy nodded and hurried to greet her sister. Jonah looked at Lawless, who nodded. Joey quickly ran after Mercy. Shadow Wolf, pointing Mercy's shotgun at Blackthorn and his sons, stepped close to Lawless.

'If somethin' goes sour,' Lawless whispered to him, 'you take the sons, I'll handle Blackthorn.'

'Agreed,' murmured the old Lakota. Keeping one eye on Blackthorn,

Lawless spoke to the five men who stood waiting beside the water trough. 'Can start puttin' out the fire now.'

'Little late for that,' one man said, eyeing the blaze. ''Sides, like you said: What's the point? C'mon,' he told the other four men, 'let's get back to our game.'

Dropping their buckets, the five men crossed the street and started back up the mountain to their cabins.

Lawless spoke to the son he held the rifle against, 'Get over there,' and pushed him toward his father and brothers. He then backed up, never taking his eyes off the Blackthorns, until he stood beside Mercy, Jonah and Cinnamon, who were arguing in loud voices.

'Button it,' he told them. Then to Cinnamon: 'These men claim you went with them willingly. That true?'

'I already asked her that,' Jonah blurted, 'and she says it is.'

'I want to hear it from her,' Lawless said. He looked hard at Cinnamon and saw that although still beautiful she had changed since he'd last seen her. It wasn't just her clothes, he realized, or the fact that her once-lustrous gold-red hair was now matted and ratty-looking. This change was internal. He saw it in her still-lovely gray-green eyes: once sultry and flutteringly flirtatious, they were now wild-looking and charged with mature defiance. Her attitude was different too: when he'd first met her she had seemed content to let her beauty do her talking; now, without saying a word, she had attitude, a look of rebelliousness that she flaunted merely by the way she stood, hands on hips, jaw thrust out, eyes filled with a boldness that warned everyone that she was liberated.

Instantly, without her answering his question, Lawless knew Blackthorn had not lied: Cinnamon *had* gone willingly, even gladly — though Lawless could not understand why.

He saw her colorless lips moving and realized she was talking. 'Yes, it's true,' he heard her say. 'I did ask them to take me with them.'

'You sure 'bout that?' he said. 'You're free of them now. You don't have to be afraid of them or worry about retaliation.'

'I'm not afraid of them,' Cinnamon said. 'Why should I be? Joey loves me and the others treat me well.'

'For God's sake,' Mercy exclaimed. 'You can't mean that!'

'But I do. What's more, when we leave here Joey's taking me to Denver and after that, maybe even San Francisco.'

'But, why would you want to go with him?' Jonah said.

'I just told you. He loves me,' Cinnamon said. She looked at Joey, who stood watching her, hangdog fashion, from nearby. 'Isn't that right, sweetheart?'

Joey nodded and smiled, showing bad teeth.

'But *we* love you, too,' Mercy said. 'Very very much.'

'I know,' Cinnamon said. 'But you don't need me, like Joey does. Oh, I know he's not much now,' she added as if he weren't present. 'But he's good at poker. Wins all the time. And he does everything I ask him to. When we get to Denver, and he wins lots of money, I'll make him into somebody. I'll buy him new clothes, get his hair cut and have the barber shave off that dreadful beard.'

She paused and studied Joey, as if seeing him as she had just described. 'You'll be surprised. He'll look very handsome. Be quite the catch.'

'I'm sure he will,' Mercy said. 'And I'm sure you'll be happy.'

'Happy and rich,' Cinnamon said. 'Then you and Jonah and Caleb can come and stay with us in San Francisco. Won't that be fun?'

Mercy tried to tell her sister that Caleb was missing and maybe drowned, but her lips refused to cooperate. She knew there was nothing left to say.

Cinnamon didn't seem to know what

else to say either. They both stood there, eyes lowered, in awkward silence. A light snow started falling. It fell silently, whitening the dirt around their feet, the flakes causing a faint hissing sound as they landed in the fire — a fire that had now burned the small wooden church to the ground.

Blackthorn stepped closer to Lawless, smirking as he said: 'Reckon you owe me'n my boys an apology, friend.'

It was the wrong thing to say.

Pent-up rage exploded inside Lawless. He whirled around and slammed the butt of his rifle against Blackthorn's jaw, smashing bone and teeth, and sending the old patriarch sprawling.

At once his sons started angrily toward Lawless. The anger that he'd carried with him all his life, anger that he'd always fought so hard to control and had promised himself that he would leave in Texas, now ran rampant. He shot the nearest son in the belly, dropping him where he stood, and was about to gun the others down when he heard someone screaming.

It was Mercy. Hurling herself at him, she begged him to stop shooting, then grabbed the barrel of his rifle and forced it downward.

He effortlessly threw her aside and aimed the Winchester at the remaining brothers. They froze in mid-stride, eyes wide with fear as they saw murder in Lawless' narrowed gray eyes and knew they were dead men.

'P-Please,' Mercy begged him from the ground. 'Don't, Ben. Please . . . I beg you . . . no more killing.'

Her voice soothed him. Still shaking, blood pounding in his ears, he fought to control his rage and . . . after what seemed like an eternity . . . gradually felt himself calming. He lowered the rifle and looked contemptuously at the brothers.

'Take your Pa an' get out of here,' he said so softly it was barely a whisper. Turning to Cinnamon, he added:

'You still got a mind to go with them, go. I'll not stop you.'

'Cinny,' Jonah said, grasping his sister's arm, 'please ... don't go ... stay with us.'

She looked at him, almost pityingly, and slowly shook her head. 'I can't,' she said. She leaned close and kissed him on the cheek. 'I'm sorry.' She looked at Mercy for a moment. 'Take care of him for me. Caleb, too.'

Before anyone could stop her, she went to Joey, tucked her arm under his, 'C'mon,' and led him back across the street.

'Make her come back,' Jonah begged Lawless. 'Please.'

'He can't,' Mercy said with a finality that silenced him. 'No one can.'

On her feet now she crossed in front of Lawless to join her brother, in doing so for a moment blocking his view of Blackthorn.

In that moment Blackthorn, who was being helped up by his two sons, pulled out the belly gun hidden beneath his undershirt and when Mercy moved out of his way, fired at Lawless.

At the same instant Shadow Wolf, seeing the gun in Blackthorn's hand, pushed Lawless out of the way. Both he and Lawless went sprawling. Lawless hit the ground, rolled over, and from his belly pumped a bullet into Blackthorn. It punched a hole in his chest, knocking him backward.

Lawless, now on his knees, fired a second shot that tore through the already dead patriarch's throat.

With no guns to fire, the brothers stood there, helpless, glaring at him, hands half-raised in surrender.

'Ben,' Mercy said, resting a calming hand on Lawless' arm. 'No more.' Then to the brothers: 'Please go. Hurry.'

They obeyed. Picking up their dead father, they carried him to the street. There, one looked back at Lawless and said: 'This ain't over, mister.' He and his brother then continued across the street and up the mountainside.

'You heard him,' Lawless said to Mercy.

'He's just talking,' she said.

'No, he means it,' Lawless said. 'I should've killed them both.'

Before Mercy could reply, there was painful grunt behind them. Both turned and saw Shadow Wolf sitting slumped over on the ground, blood seeping between his fingers as he clasped his belly.

Lawless quickly kneeled beside him. He started to say something but the old Lakota looked at him and shook his head. He then smiled at Mercy, as she too kneeled beside him. A moment later Jonah joined them, alarmed as he saw the blood on the Indian's hand.

'Do not worry yourselves,' Shadow Wolf said to them in perfect English. 'It is my time.'

'Cut it out,' Lawless told him. 'You ain't goin' to die, you old fake. You got too much whiskey comin'.'

Shadow Wolf grinned, showing the one front tooth still remaining in his gums. 'You will drink it for me,' he said to Lawless. He coughed, grimacing in pain, and blood ran from his mouth. 'I must leave you now,' he said weakly. 'Takuskanskan calls me to eternity.'

'Jesus Christ,' Lawless said angrily, 'don't feed me that guardian spirit crap. Not in this day and age. You're goin' to be fine.'

'A pact is a pact,' Shadow Wolf said — and died.

Lawless caught the old Lakota as his body slumped forward. 'Damn you,' he said, shaking him. 'Damn you an' damn that goddamn stupid pact!'

He looked at Mercy, and at Jonah, and saw they were both crying. He sighed, more frustrated than anything else, and then putting his arms around them pulled them close to him.

'We better find shelter for tonight,' he told them.

'That old brown building we passed on our way in looked empty,' Mercy said, sniffing back her tears. 'Maybe we could sleep in there.'

'Good idea,' Lawless said. 'Then first thing tomorrow, we'll head back down to the river an' start lookin' for Caleb.'

Mercy smiled and brushed her fringe back. 'I'd like that, Ben.'

Jonah looked doubtfully at them. 'Y-You really think he's still alive?'

'Son,' Lawless said gently. 'Would I waste time lookin' for him if I didn't?'

THE END

VALLEY OF THE GUNS

Rick Dalmas

Zack Clay is looking for a quiet life, but he hasn't reckoned on range-grabbers Dutch Haas and Burt Helidon bringing in sundry gunfighters to hassle him. Clay meets fists and boots with the same, gunsmoke with gunsmoke. In the end, they hang a badge on him. Then things really hot up in Benbow. But the hustlers, gunslingers, the wild trailmen and townsmen who put dollars before citizens all find that stubborn Zack Clay won't go down without a fight . . .

THE SKULL OF IRON EYES

Rory Black

In a remote valley, led by Will Hayes, six miners strike pay dirt. A fortune in golden nuggets is hidden in the dense landscape. The only obstacle to prevent their taking it back to civilization is a small, isolated tribe of natives, but Hayes has a dastardly plan . . . However, after they ruthlessly kill a child, her body is found by the infamous bounty hunter Iron Eyes. And he vows to discover who killed her — and see justice done . . .